a new kind of dreaming

Anthony Eaton was born in 1972 in a town which later burned to the ground in a volcanic eruption. He has been known to describe this event as "just typical". Generally, though, he is a lot more cheerful and spends his time writing books and occasionally fishing. While he is yet to catch anything larger than a herring, he has high expectations. He has also been known to exercise sporadically ...

In 1997 he met Gary Crew at a writer's workshop, and decided to become a writer. *The Darkness*, his first novel, was published in 2000 and won the West Australian Premier's Award for young adult fiction. His second novel, *A New Kind of Dreaming* was a Children's Book Council of Australia Notable Australian Book and was also included in the prestigious International Youth Library Selection of Notable books (White Ravens) catalogue. In 2002 he released *Nathan Nuttboard Hits the Beach* — his first book for younger readers.

Also by the same author

The Darkness
Fireshadow

Younger Reader
Nathan Nuttboard Hits the Beach
The Girl in the Cave

a new
kind
of
dreaming

Anthony
Eaton

University of Queensland Press

First published 2001 by University of Queensland Press
Box 6042, St Lucia, Queensland 4067 Australia
Reprinted 2002, 2003, 2004 (twice), 2005, 2006, 2008

www.uqp.uq.edu.au

Typeset by University of Queensland Press
Printed in Australia by McPherson's Printing Group

This project has been assisted by
the Commonwealth Government through
the Australia Council, its arts funding
and advisory body.

Cataloguing in Publication Data
National Library of Australia

Eaton, Anthony, 1972–   .
    A new kind of dreaming.

    I. Title.

A823.3

ISBN 978 0 7022 3228 2

*To Nick & Sue; siblings
and great friends.*

Acknowledgments

The saying on page (178), *A friend always leaves a trail*, can be found in Stephen Muecke's foreword to the 1992 edition of the novel *Wildcat Falling* by Mudrooroo Narrogin. It is attributed to David Unaipon.

Australians are surrounded by ocean and ambushed from behind by desert — a war of mystery on two fronts. What worries us about the sea and the desert? Is it scale, or simply silence?

Tim Winton
Land's Edge

If you don't learn about this place and love this land, then your spirit will be restless and you will feel like you don't belong.

Boori (Monty) Pryor
Maybe Tomorrow

Prelude:

Awakening

The boat was dead.

It drifted, alone, across the oily swells of the deep, showing none of the signs of life one would normally expect from a ship at sea. No feet walked its deck, the throb and pulse of diesel engines no longer shook its timbers, the surge and sway of the hull against the waves was no longer a sensation felt by anyone aboard, except perhaps ghosts. In the small wheelhouse mounted over the stern, the wheel swung uselessly from port to starboard and then back again, spiralling endlessly without a guiding hand.

In the early afternoon sun it cast a sinister silhouette, black against the silver glare of sun on water, listing heavily to one side as it rolled abeam through the troughs and peaks of the seemingly eternal Indian ocean.

The six men fishing from their cabin cruiser a couple of kilometres away didn't spot the boat itself. Initially they noticed the thick black cloud of seabirds that wheeled in the air above it. Boobies, terns and petrels, attracted by the prospect of easy food. Only when they turned towards the distant feeding flock did the men notice the dark shape on the surface of the water.

"What d'ya reckon that is?"

"Dunno. Let's check it out, eh?"

The cruiser lifted across the surface as the powerful inboards roared into life beneath the fish locker.

The men were young, most in their early twenties. Only one looked a little older, perhaps twenty-seven or eight, and he stood alone in the stern, apart from the others who gathered around the helm. The shape began to resolve itself into a lifeless hulk that wallowed on the waves, driven slowly by the sea towards the distant north-western Australian coastline, thirty-five kilometres away over the southern horizon.

Coming closer, the driver eased back on the throttles and the vessel settled into the water, describing a slow circle around the mysterious craft, keeping about twenty metres away. All six men were silent.

Next to their sleek aluminum and fibreglass cruiser, the timber boat looked old and unwieldy, barely seaworthy. Its high, raked bow led back in a long sweeping arc to a boxy wheelhouse perched precariously above the square stern. The men shouted, but their calls echoed unanswered across the water.

Passing downwind of the silent boat, the stench of decay reached out from the drifting vessel and assaulted their nostrils, making stomachs heave and eyes water. One of the men, the youngest, leaned over the side and threw up violently. For a few seconds he lay across the rail retching, the roll of the boat bringing his face to within centimetres of the surface of the water.

"Look!"

"Holy shit!"

A black fin sliced through the water, and then another. In seconds, the sea was boiling with lithe, dark shapes snapping and twisting in all directions.

"Sharks."

"Yeah. You see hundreds of them in these waters. Not usually all in the one place, though. I've never seen 'em like this."

"What's attractin' them, do you think?"

The fishermen stared at the drifting hulk.

"I'm gonna radio Coastwatch and get 'em to send a boat out."

The helmsman reached for the VHF radio built into the helm console.

"Hang on a minute." The older man, standing alone in the stern, took a step forward. All eyes turned to him. He hadn't spoken loudly, just the opposite, and yet the effect of his words on the other five members of the fishing party was electric. The helmsman's hand stopped mid-air, halfway to the microphone.

"Get us up alongside. I want to have a look around first."

Silence ...

"You sure?"

"Yeah. Better check things out and see what the deal is."

No one moved, no one spoke.

"Don't be an idiot." The man who had vomited hauled himself back to his feet.

"An idiot?" The figure in the stern arched one eyebrow slightly, questioningly. On the bronzed face, the gesture was sinister and threatening. Even so, the younger man refused to back down.

"That's what I said. Let's just call the Coastwatch and get the hell out of here."

"What's the matter, Mike? You scared?"

"Bugger off! Of course I'm not scared. I just ..." His voice trailing away, Mike looked down at the deck, uncomfortably aware of the level gaze of the man in the stern.

"Good then. You can come across with me."

Mike continued to stare at the deck, unwilling to meet the challenge behind the older man's words, but in the end he was unable to refuse to do so.

"Whatever. Let's just make it quick, okay." His voice was little more than a hoarse whisper.

The man in the stern smiled. A cold, hard smile, then nodded to the helmsman.

"Take us alongside, Gerry."

With no engines and no steering, the larger wooden boat was unpredictable and dangerous in its movements. It surged up and then dropped away from the smaller powerboat with little or no warning. Gerry drifted the cruiser down towards the wooden hulk while the crew hung rubber fenders off the side of their own craft to hold them safely apart. The stench wafted over to them, even from upwind, and a couple of the men had to fight the urge to gag and cough. Mike looked into the narrowing gap of indigo water between the two boats, uncomfortably aware of the dark, streamlined shapes cruising silently below.

"Not nervous, are we?"

Mike could only shake his head in reply.

"Good then. I'll go first."

When the roll of the two boats brought their rails roughly level, the man leapt easily across the dark water and onto the timber deck of the dead boat. Although he was a large man, tall and solidly built, he made the jump with the grace and agility of a jungle cat. Once aboard, he disappeared towards the wheelhouse.

Perched on the rail, Mike stood a few seconds longer, feeling his mates' stares at his back. He knew exactly what they were thinking. Below him a torpedo-shaped black and silver shark broke the surface of the water with its dorsal fin.

"Look, Mike ..."

Mike took a deep breath and leapt. Everything slowed. Gravity seemed to settle upon him, drawing him inexorably down towards the waiting sharks.

And then he was across, sprawled in an undignified heap, splinters from the deck driving into the palms of his hands. When he looked back towards the cruiser, his mates were standing still and silent, watching as he climbed to his feet.

Gerry spun the helm, and the cruiser pulled away from the splintering hulk.

The air on board was foul. Even on the open deck the scent of decay tainted every breath. Mike's stomach heaved again, but all he could manage was a dry heave. From aft came a soft, derisive laugh.

"Made it, did you? Took your time all right. Didn't think you'd have the guts."

Mike shrugged. The big man was watching him through the shattered remains of the wheelhouse window.

"Come and have a look at this."

The boat had taken on water and leaned permanently to one side. On the bigger swells it would roll slowly and lazily, to the point where the lower rail came within a few centimetres of dipping beneath the surface of the water.

Hundreds of pencil-thin beams of light streamed into the wheelhouse through small, neat holes in the wooden walls. The simple instrument panel looked like it had been attacked with an axe. Broken glass and splinters of wood littered the floor. A dark brown stain on the rear bulkhead ran down and across through the far door to the lower rail at the side of the boat.

"Is that ...?"

A nod.

"Yep. Something real nasty went down on this wreck."

"Shit!"

"I'm going to have a look below."

The other man vanished though a hatchway. Alone in the wheelhouse, Mike glanced nervously about. Everything on board was still, the only sounds the creaking of the timbers, the sloshing of water in the bilge, and the cries of the seabirds circling endlessly above.

The smell and the close atmosphere inside the cabin were too much for him. He stepped back out onto the deck. Smashed wooden crates and piles of rope and netting were strewn everywhere. With the brightness and intensity of the sunlight, the hatchways down into the belly of the boat seemed to lead into a black pit of darkness.

"Hey, get down here!"

"What?"

"You'll see. Get down here."

If the smell was bad up on deck, down it was doubly so. It drifted with a sweet, cloying and yet evil scent that pervaded every part of Mike's thought processes. The air had substance, settling and clinging to his skin and clothes.

Mike closed his eyes for a few seconds, willing his stomach to settle. Feeling a little calmer he re-opened them, to be confronted by a scene of pure horror.

They were gathered together up in the bow. Forty or fifty of them, piled on top of one another — men, women and children. A nightmare of humanity. Bodies twisted into grotesque forms, arms and legs angled in all directions in the semi-darkness.

Mercifully, lack of light hid specific details. Mike stared, long enough to take in the expressions of agony and fear on the faces, the ragged bullet holes in chests and limbs, the heads half blown away, and the stained deck beneath the gruesome pile.

This time there was no containing the wave of nausea that overcame him; he clawed his way back up the stairs, into the sunlight, and dashed for the side rail.

As he lay prone, spewing evil-tasting yellow bile into dark blue waters, a hand grabbed his shoulder.

Mike continued vomiting, assuming that the grip was the other man wanting to get away. Bugger him! If the dumb bastard wanted to get off, then he could wait.

Eventually Mike straightened, his guts still cramping from the exertion. The grip on his shoulder had taken on a strange insistent quality, some strength he hadn't noticed before.

"Let up! You're hurting!"

Mike found himself staring into the hollow eyes of a walking corpse.

Open sores gaped on the skin of the emaciated figure. A tattered sarong clung around his waist, but there was barely enough of it to cover him properly. In his right hand a rusted machete hung limp and heavy, its pitted blade glinting dully in the afternoon sun.

For ten or fifteen seconds the two men stood locked in motionless silence. At the edges of Mike's consciousness, the afternoon light, the boat, the ocean, everything dissolved away into nothingness; all that remained were the eyes of the other man — two hollow orbs of madness and dark desperation which trapped him, pulling him in, sucking him down. He was caught. Drawn into a long tunnel of pain and horror — no end in sight. The sensation was one of falling — of being swamped, engulfed and surrounded as the gleaming black insanity behind those eyes invaded his thoughts and drew him to itself.

Abruptly, the spell was broken. A wet thump, and the man stiffened and folded in a heap on the deck. He tried to speak, uttering some soft, unintelligible sounds before his eyes rolled back in their sockets. His body twitched a couple of times and then was still.

Over the body stood the other man from the fishing boat. In his hand was an iron bar, its end stained a bloody red, a strange expression on his face — half panic, half triumph.

"Oh my God! Elliot, what did you do?"

The larger man shrugged he was visibly shaken and trying not to show his fear, but when he spoke there was a note of pride, of arrogant confidence in his voice.

"What does it look like? He was gonna kill you, you dumb bugger."

"That's bullshit!"

"Come on, he had a machete."

"Yeah, but ..."

"Don't be a dickhead, mate. I just saved your life."

The crumpled form lay motionless, a dark stain already spreading on the deck behind its head.

"Is he dead?"

"I should bloody hope so. I hit him hard enough."

"What are we gonna do? Let's call the others and get out of here."

"Hang on a minute." The larger man scratched his chin, thinking. "It seems to me that one way or the other this old hulk is headed for the Aussie coastline."

"So? Who cares?"

"I do. It's only a matter of time before someone else finds it, right?"

Other than a mute nod, Mike offered no reply.

"Well then, the last thing we need is for someone to come poking around and discover that this guy died on deck from a blow to the head, when everyone else on board was shot down below. Hell, with modern forensics, they'll soon work out that he died a few days later than all the others, and then there'll be all sorts of awkward questions."

"Fine, but I don't see what we can do. There's —"

He didn't get an opportunity to finish. Without any further discussion the larger man reached down, grabbed the body by one arm and began to drag it towards the lee rail.

"What are you doing, Elliot?"

"Shut up, Mike, and give me a hand." Reaching the far side of the deck, he struggled to heave the body upright. The dead man was little more than a skeleton, but he was still heavy and awkward to lug up off the slanting deck.

"Hang on! We haven't even checked to see if he's dead yet."

"If he isn't then he soon will be. Now give me a hand."

"But ..."

"I said, give me a hand here." Some softly spoken suggestion behind the words made it impossible to argue. In a daze, Mike seized the body by the other arm and hauled it up and over the side.

It hit the water with very little splash, sliding gently into the surface and then floating for a second or two before the first of the sharks, attracted by the blood, lunged from the deep. Within seconds, the water was a seething frenzy.

"There." Elliot took a couple of steps back and wiped his hands on his pants. "That solves one problem."

Mike looked up, amazed and frightened; Elliot was smiling. The same hard, cold, emotionless smile that he'd witnessed before. A smile that touched the corners of his mouth but had no impact on his eyes.

"Now then, Mikey boy" — Elliot clapped him on the back, hard. "Let's see about organising a tow rope of some sort."

The other boat was still some distance away — out of the smell. Moving across to the other rail, Elliot waved their friends in the fishing boat back across.

"Here they come. Oh, and Mikey? This'll all have to be our little secret, eh?" He turned his attention back to the approaching cruiser, while Mike struggled to get himself under control before his mates arrived.

Neither noticed the pair of eyes watching them from under a pile of rope and netting strewn in the bow.

Arrival

ONE

As the coach pulled back out onto the highway, a figure stood alone in the thick red cloud it left behind. The desert breeze drifted the dust across towards the town and Jamie Riley looked around, taking in his first sight of Port Barren.

"Shit."

He'd expected to hate the place, right from the moment that the judge had passed sentence. No disappointment there, Port Barren was a hole. A hot, dusty, dry hole with flies. It was only eight in the morning, but the temperature was already in the thirties. Jamie's tee-shirt clung to his skin. "No wonder Eddie started laughing."

It seemed like weeks, not days, ago that they'd sat on opposite sides of the thick safety glass, shouting to be heard through the few small holes, and Jamie had told his brother about the court's decision to send him to Port Barren. Eddie had cracked up. It had taken about ten minutes for him to stop laughing long enough to continue talking.

"Jeez mate, Port Barren. And I thought I'd got the rough end of the stick being banged up in here."

"Ah, it won't be that bad." Jamie affected his best "I don't give a damn" attitude. It had no impact on his brother, though. Eddie knew him too well.

"Yeah, right mate. And I'm having a ball in here — the warden's making me a cake for my birthday." He chuckled. That was the problem with Eddie — life was one big joke. Even getting stuck in prison, or packed off by the court to some shithole in the middle of the desert was good for a laugh.

"Bugger off. I reckon I'll probably like the place."

"Yeah? You don't remember it then, do you?" Eddie gave him a look.

"Remember what?"

"Port Barren. You've been there before, you know." *little kid*

"Yeah. Right." Eddie — always trying to put one over you.

"Nah, seriously mate. When you were a little tacker 'bout two or three years old. Mum took both of us up there one time."

Mum. Jamie didn't remember much about her. She'd died when he was four. A long time ago.

"Why'd she do that?"

"Dunno. She never really told us. I musta been six or seven. We drove about four days solid just to get there." Eddie paused, recollecting faded memories. "Seem to remember Mum saying she had family up that way."

"Family?" For as long as Jamie could recall, his family had been Eddie, who was locked away now for five to seven years, and their dad, usually too pissed to worry about anything, particularly the boys. "Don't remember anyone sayin' anything like that."

"You wouldn't, would you? You were still too young when Mum ..." Eddie stopped. Their mother was a delicate issue for both of them.

Every now and then Jamie tried to remember his mum but all he could ever come up with was this idea of a sad woman. That was about it — someone sad. There were a few vague memories, like shadows. He could remember her lugging boxes around during one of their many moves, and playing a singing game with them in the car on one of their country trips. What he couldn't remember was her smell, what she felt like, being hugged. Anything like that. A few years ago it used to bother him, not being able to remember her, but nowadays he didn't let it.

It was different for Eddie though, Jamie thought. He could remember a lot about Mum. It meant he missed her. A lot more than he ever let on. *he is sensitive on the inside*

He stared hard at his brother slouching in his chair on the other side of the glass and wondered if Eddie looked anything like their mum. He sure didn't look much like Dad — that was one thing he could be glad about.

The guard at the far end of the room coughed a little and glanced pointedly at his watch. Even through the thick glass Eddie caught the gesture.

"Arsehole."

"Yeah. Anyway ..." Jamie trailed off. Suddenly he wasn't sure what to say. He didn't really know when the two of them would see each other again. Eddie and he had never been particularly affectionate, but even so —

"You better get a move on."

"Yeah, I guess."

"Don't wanna miss the bus." Eddie grinned again.

"That's not a bad idea. You reckon I'd get away with it?" Jamie tried to smile back.

"Go on. Get lost then."

Jamie stood slowly. For a couple of seconds he stared at Ed. Rocking backwards on the old wooden school chair in his bloody ugly green prison uniform. Both of them were doing their best to appear as cool as possible. Finally, Jamie gave a small nod and turned to leave.

"Hey, Jamie mate."

"Yeah?" He stopped.

"You take care, little brother. You hear me?" *isn't he going away?*

"Yeah, don't worry, I will."

"Nah, I mean it — you stay out of trouble. When I get out we'll do something straight."

"When'll that be?"

"Not sure exactly." Eddie swung slowly to his feet. "I'll come and find you, okay?"

"Sure mate." On impulse Jamie reached out and put his hand on the glass. The palms were sweaty, and the glass felt cold and solid. Eddie gave the partition a slap. A high-five through two centimetres of reinforced safety glass.

"See ya."

"Be good."

And now here he was. Standing in a cloud of dust by the side of Highway One, five hundred kilometres the other side of anywhere.

"Shit."

Slowly Jamie turned. He took in his first view of the place that would be his home for the next two years. It wasn't much to look at. A few fibro bungalows scattered between thin patches of scrub and joined by red dirt roads. Everything was coated with dust, and in the early morning light the whole town took on a dirty pink glow. [ ] *are they in Arizona*

Opposite the bus stop crouched a larger building. A verandah ran along the side facing the highway, and as he stared a shape detached itself from the shade beneath it and started across the shoulder of the road towards him. *thats what they make blacktop with*

It was a woman. He had to squint to make out the figure through the shimmering heat rising off the tarmac. She wore a long, patterned skirt that flicked around in the dust at her feet. *author*

She approached slowly, evenly, sizing him up as she paced across the hot tarmac.

"You must be Jamie."

"Me? Nah, sorry. You must be lookin' for someone else."

A momentary expression of concern flickered across her face. Spot the social worker. It had been one of Jamie's

? spelled wrong?

favourite games back home. He'd been good at it too. On a Friday night he and his mates used to hang out around the central train station, waiting until either the cops or the social workers turned up. Either way there was entertainment to be had. He'd have spotted this one a mile away. She had that burnt-out hippie look they all seemed to pick up. He let her worry, enjoying the uneasy silence. When he'd had enough, he let her off.

"Yeah. You got me — I'm Jamie Riley."

"Oh, right. I thought you must have been." A tight smile. "I'm Lorraine." She held out her hand. Jamie stared at it. The *new* skin was clean and pink, the nails neatly trimmed. On the end *(word)* of the sun-browned, weathered arm, it looked out of place. He made no attempt to take it and eventually the woman let it fall back to her side.

"I'm the district officer for this area. I'll be keeping an eye out for you during your stay."

He'd learnt the best way to deal with people like this long ago. Simply shut up, let them talk themselves out. Most people didn't like silence, so if you let them try to fill in the gaps they'd give away more than they intended. This one turned out to be different. She let the silence hang in the air between them for a full minute while she looked him up and down, taking in the faded jeans and the stained Jim Beam tee-shirt. Under her level stare, Jamie found himself feeling uncomfortable, unconsciously shifting his weight from one foot to the other — a gesture of weakness he'd never usually permit himself to display, least of all to a social worker.

Finally, without another word, she spun around and started back across the highway.

"Well, come on."

Grabbing his backpack, which had been dumped in the dirt beside him when he got off the bus, Jamie slouched onto the road.

Halfway across the highway, with the heat rising from the

black tarmac like a physical presence, Jamie stopped dead. A feeling of cold gripped him, coming from right down inside, making him tremble. Something bad, something evil had reached out and touched him as he crossed the road. His shoulders felt tight and heavy, his breathing became shallow and forced, and he fought back a wave of nausea. He couldn't explain it, but he had this instant, eerie feeling that something was very wrong with Port Barren.

[handwritten margin notes: like in the pirate scene]

Lorraine had stopped on the far side of the highway.

"You okay?"

Jamie shook his head to start himself thinking again.

"Yeah, I'm fine."

He'd caught up to her by the time she reached the verandah of the long prefab, and they walked up the three steps together.

"This is admin," said Lorraine. "It's sort of the centre of town. The mining company has its offices down that end, and this half of the building is the council office. I keep a desk here too, for when I'm about."

"You're not always here?"

She laughed.

"In Port Barren? No way. This place isn't big enough to warrant a full-time social worker. I drive across from Karratha two or three times a week, just to touch base."

"With who?"

A sideways glance.

"You for one."

Jamie went quiet again and followed Lorraine into the council offices. After the heat outside, the interior of the prefab was so cold it made him gasp. Lorraine noticed the goose bumps that prickled all over him.

"They keep the air-con running all the time. Not a bad thing either — gets pretty warm this time of year."

"What's it like in summer then?" When Jamie had left the city, way down south, it had been freezing cold and pouring with rain — the dead of winter. If this was what winter was like in Port Barren, he couldn't imagine it during the hot weather.

"Summer?" Lorraine laughed again. "This is the far north Jamie, there's no summer. Only the wet and the dry."

"Eh?"

"You'll see. Right now though, we're in the middle of the dry season."

"When's the wet?"

"Still about a month away. Hard to say exactly. Some years it seems to come earlier than others."

"Does it get a bit cooler then?"

"Not much, just a lot more humid." *that seems bad*

"Great."

While they talked she'd led him between three or four desks, past a couple of partitioned offices and into a cubbyhole tucked away at one end of the room. Jamie guessed there was a desk somewhere under the piles of books and paper that littered the tiny space.

"Sorry about the mess." Lorraine eased herself into a chair on the other side of the biggest pile of books. "Take a seat."

An old wooden chair stood against the wall behind him. Jamie pulled it to the edge of the desk and sat down. Lorraine lifted the top books off the pile and dumped them on the floor where they kicked up a small cloud of red dust. Jamie watched the cloud gradually settle back to the floor.

"That's better. At least now I can see you."

Jamie didn't reply and the social worker studied him again for a few more seconds before plucking a slim manila folder off the top of one pile. *what is he doing at this camp*

"Now, let's see. James Riley, seventeen, father missing, mother deceased, one brother currently serving a maximum security sentence for armed robbery and theft."

Jamie yawned. There was nothing in that file that he didn't already know, and he didn't want to give this woman the impression that he cared in the slightest what she knew about him.

Lorraine continued reading aloud.

"Referred into custody of the Department for Social Services at age twelve after repeated shoplifting offences, five foster homes in the following five years. Arrested in August of this year in the passenger seat of a stolen car. Sentenced to two years in juvenile remand by the Children's Court, but after an appeal by Ms Karen Kernol of the DSS this sentence was commuted to two years isolated care." *?whats that?*

Hearing the last six years of his life summed up so quickly and emotionlessly made Jamie feel a little uncomfortable, but he was careful not to let any expression into his face.

Lorraine leaned back in her chair and looked at him.

"You're a pretty lucky guy."

"Lucky? Being sent to this dump?"

"It's better than remand." *I agree with her*

"Dunno about that."

"Trust me, it is. You ever been inside a prison?"

"Yeah, plenty of times. Visited my brother every couple of months."

"No, I mean really inside. Not just the visitor's room."

"Nah. Eddie reckons it's not too bad, though. Lots of free time, pool table, even cable TV."

Lorraine's steady gaze held his for a few seconds, and then she said, "Eddie."

Calmly, she closed his file and dropped it back onto the desk. Without hesitation, she plucked another folder, identical to his own, from the top of a different pile. While she leafed through the pages, searching, Jamie took the opportunity to study her. He guessed she was somewhere in her forties. Long stringy brown hair hung right down to the middle of her back. A pair of thick reading glasses perched on the end of her nose and she wore an old, faded Greenpeace tee-shirt. Her skin had that look of someone who's lived too long in a hot, dry climate — dark and kind of creased.

Unlike a lot of the social workers he'd dealt with in the past, this one, despite the tired hippy façade, gave the impression that she shouldn't be messed around. She seemed to have all the answers.

"Did Eddie tell you about the fights?"

? What does that mean

"Eh?"

"In the two years he's been inside, your brother's been admitted to the prison hospital five times."

"What for?"

"To get patched up. From beatings."

"Nah. He woulda told me."

"It's all in here." She waved the folder.

For the first time since sitting down, Jamie felt disconcerted. None of the other social workers had ever known any details about Eddie. They'd known he existed, of course, and that he was in prison, but as far as Jamie was aware that was about all they were ever told. He'd always assumed it was all they were allowed to know.

"How'd you get that?"

"What?"

"Eddie's file."

Lorraine threw him a strange smile.

"I've got my contacts." *go into great detail*

She didn't elaborate and Jamie retreated back into silence. After a second or two she returned her attention to the folder.

"They broke his nose last time."

"Who did?"

"He won't say. One of the gangs probably. Prison's full of men with grudges."

"He didn't tell me."

"He wouldn't, would he? You're his little brother. You look up to him."

"Eddie's not like that." *And neither am I*, he almost added.

▲ 23

"You'd be surprised, Jamie. Things like respect and family become pretty important to guys once they're locked up. Particularly for men like Eddie. It's all they've got left to hold on to."

Lorraine pulled something from the file and passed it to Jamie. She had to rise slightly to reach across the mess without starting an avalanche. It was a photo. Of Eddie. That in itself was strange — Ed had always had a thing about photos, he hated being in them. He'd never let anyone take a snapshot of him if he could help it. For a few seconds Jamie studied the image — the black eyes, the twisted nose and the bloodstained prison tee-shirt. Lorraine watched him closely, looking to see his reaction.

"Oh man." Jamie was quiet, taking it in. "Why didn't he say something?"

"What could you have done?"

Another pause.

"Do you see why I say you're lucky?"

Jamie shook his head. His mind was reeling with shock and anger and fear for his brother. He barely heard Lorraine speaking, but forced himself back to her words — it was the best way to keep the emotions from taking over.

"Jamie, you're seventeen now. With your record you could easily have been in there with your brother. A two-year term now would have meant at least twelve months in the adult prison."

"So?"

"So you're incredibly lucky that your case worker managed to talk the judge into releasing you to isolated care. You mess up again and it's prison for you. Not just juvenile remand, but full-on prison. You think about that. I don't know Eddie but I'm guessing he's no pushover, and even so they've managed to put him in hospital five times. Imagine what would happen to a seventeen-year-old." She paused. "This is it, Jamie. This is your last chance."

Silence filled the space between them. Jamie tried to shrug off what she'd just said: All his life social workers had been telling him that this was his last chance, and so far he'd proved them wrong every time. Deep inside him, however, a tight little bundle of nerves told him that in this case what Lorraine was saying was really true. He listened as Lorraine kept talking.

"What I'm saying is this — don't mess up here. Go to school, meet me every week, don't play up on Archie ..."

"Archie?" Jamie interrupted.

"You'll meet him in a few minutes. You'll be staying with him. Give him a chance and I think you'll like him. You actually remind me of him a little."

The hum of the air-conditioners filled the break in the conversation. Jamie's mind was turning over what Lorraine had said. *She has no idea about Eddie,* he thought. She believed she knew everything about everybody. Jamie reckoned he knew his brother pretty well. Still, he remembered that last meeting. Eddie had been different, sort of tired and sad. Not the old Ed at all.

Jamie broke the silence. "Is that it?"

The social worker looked up. "Is what it?"

"This interview."

Lorraine stared. "I'd like to know what your plans are for your stay."

"Plans?"

"You need to have some sort of goals."

Jamie gave a hollow laugh.

"What's the point? I'm not goin' anywhere in a hurry, am I?"

"Even so —" She broke off, looking up. "Archie, come on in."

TWO

Jamie twisted in his seat to get a good look at the person who *[handwritten: to see into the future]* was going to be his host for the (foreseeable) future. He expected to see someone like the foster parents they'd always dumped him with back in the city — some well-meaning, church-going, middle-class do-gooder. He'd hated them all: people who thought they could change the world by changing him. That was what the social services people never understood — that for the foster parents it was always some kind of mission, a competition, with them on the side of good and Jamie being the forces of darkness and evil. It was a competition Jamie had become very good at winning.

Not this time, though, Jamie thought, as he examined the *[handwritten: meets Archie]* man standing in the doorway. *This guy's gonna be different.*

In his mind he'd already decided that he could deal with Lorraine; he reckoned he had her number. Just say what she wanted to hear, look like he was staying out of everyone's way and she'd go off back to Karratha happy. Looking at Archie, though, Jamie had the feeling that he wouldn't be so easy to fool. For a start he was old. Probably double the age of any of the other foster parents. Jamie figured he must be in his seventies, possibly even his eighties; it was hard to tell.

He had an ageless appearance, the look of someone who's seen a great deal, and hasn't let any of it worry him particularly. *looks very wise*

The old man took a small step into the room, nodding to Lorraine. There was nowhere for him to sit so he propped himself against a wall.

"Jamie, this is Archie, who you'll be staying with. His place is only a couple of minutes walk from here." * *Staying at a house*

The old man looked straight at him. His eyes, which had been half-closed, were an almost electric blue, in stark contrast to his dark, sun-browned skin and shock of white hair. Jamie felt as though the old man's eyes were not looking at his face or his appearance but were searing their way into his mind, into his soul. He sat paralysed, unable to speak or move or even to tear his eyes away from that steady, piercing gaze.

"Archie, any problems getting the house set up?" Lorraine was still talking, seemingly unaware of Jamie's reaction.

Archie didn't reply, just turned back to Lorraine and gave a slight nod. This seemed to satisfy her. Released abruptly from Archie's stare, Jamie felt himself sag. *Seems like a shady guy?*

"Good. You guys might as well get going then. I'm sure that after four days on a bus Jamie's anxious to settle in and stretch out a little."

It took a couple of seconds for Jamie to realise that she was speaking to him; he was still recovering from that searching stare. Why did he feel that in that brief look the old man had learnt everything that he needed to know about him?

"Huh? Oh, yeah. Whatever."

"Well then." Lorraine rose and started around the side of the desk. Archie led them out of the cubbyhole; he seemed to know his way around. "I'll be staying in town overnight so that I can get you settled at school in the morning. There are only a few students, and most of them are pretty young, I'm afraid; but Mr Scott is a nice guy — you'll get on well with

school teacher?

him. I'll meet you here in front of admin at about eight tomorrow morning, okay?"

"Yeah."

"Good." She opened the door to the verandah. "I'll see you then. Thanks again Archie, I really appreciate this."

The only sign he gave that he had heard her was another of those almost imperceptible nods, and then Archie made his way down the steps, turned left, and started across the hard-packed ground. The old man was barefoot. Jamie began to follow, but Lorraine stopped him as he reached the bottom step.

"Jamie." He turned. "Remember what we spoke about, okay? Your last chance."

"Yeah, okay."

The boy stepped out from the shade. The heat struck him violently, like being hit in the face. It seemed to be rising up out of the very ground. After the frigid conditions inside admin, it was like stepping from a freezer into a blast furnace. A brief dizziness swept over him, but he breathed deeply and the moment passed. Up ahead Archie was walking away through the haze without looking back, his bare feet not even leaving an impression on the hard red earth.

Jamie almost yelled at the old man to wait up, but caught himself just in time. The last thing he wanted to do was let them know how out of place he felt here. That would be giving them far too much of an advantage over him, especially this early on. Something was disconcerting him, messing up his thinking. He'd have to be careful. Slinging his bag onto his back, Jamie started to traipse through the dirt. He didn't try to close the distance, just kept Archie in sight and followed.

They continued in this fashion for about ten minutes. It felt like an eternity. The dust quickly filled Jamie's eyes and mouth, settling on his hair and sticking to his skin. The burning sun seared his uncovered arms and he itched inside his tight tee-shirt. Determined, however, not to give this old man with the strange eyes the satisfaction of thinking that he was winning, Jamie stayed silent.

Something made him look up. Ahead, the wiry figure of the old man still plodded steadily through the shimmering heat, but now there was another figure too. A slightly built man, taller than Archie, and yet somehow less substantial, weaved his way towards them, staggering down the middle of the road.

The man in the street and Archie passed one another. There might have been some brief exchange, but if there was the words were kept from his hearing by distance and the desert breeze. Archie gave no sign of stopping, no sign of hearing anything. He simply kept walking.

The man wore the khaki uniform of the country police. It was crumpled and stained as though he'd slept in it, and covered in dust and dirt. The cop was clearly drunk, and Jamie couldn't help glancing at his watch — nine o'clock in the morning. The policeman, noticing Jamie for the first time, stopped in the middle of the road and stood unsteadily for a second or two before finding his voice.

"Hey!" His voice was slurred and uneven. Jamie ignored him, taking his cue from Archie, and kept up a steady pace.

"Hey, mate!"

Jamie kept waking, being careful not to cast even a slight glance in the man's direction. Drunk or not, a cop was not someone he wanted to mess with. The drunk's voice floated after him.

"You better watch out, mate. Don't say I didn't warn you. You watch out."

Resisting the urge to reply, Jamie walked on until the drunk cop's voice faded into the distance behind him. The encounter had shaken him, and he was relieved to see Archie stop at one of the houses on the very edge of town and turn in through the gate. He didn't check to see whether Jamie was alright,

what is that mean?

or even following. The old man walked up the red dirt path, climbed the steps, crossed the verandah and disappeared through a torn flyscreen into the darkness of the house.

Reaching the end of the path Jamie paused. The house was unpainted and transmitted a feeling of lived-in disrepair. Rust marks streaked the metal roof, and the guttering at the edges of the verandah was pulling away. Jamie took in the neighbourhood. There wasn't a lot to see. A few similar houses, a couple of them abandoned judging by the broken windows and holes in the walls. Over the road lay the rest of Port Barren, dotted across the flat scrubby plain towards the sea, and in the other direction, to the south behind Archie's place, stretched the empty expanse of the Great Sandy Desert. Not a sound reached him. The whole place rested in a kind of deathly, unnatural stillness.

Uncertain whether it was okay to just walk in, Jamie took a couple of hesitant steps. Behind the flyscreen, the front door was wide open, a rectangle of cool darkness. It looked inviting from where Jamie stood, slowly turning to toast in the blazing glare of the morning sun.

A slight breeze stirred the air, and the flyscreen swung on its hinges. The heat and dust gave the morning a shimmering, surreal quality, like watching a film that has been slowed down and is slightly out of focus. Jamie approached the steps on unsteady legs, grabbing at the handrail for support. A sense of uneasiness and foreboding had settled upon him the moment he'd stepped off the bus, and now it permeated every fibre of his being. It was as though some unsettling energy was rising from the landscape, oozing up out of the dusty ground and decrepit shacks, drifting in the dirty, glowing air. Dizziness picked him up and carried him. ⚹ Same feeling

Jamie gripped the handrail, his knuckles white, his palms as sweaty, as wave after wave of nausea swept over him. His before legs refused to move, to climb the three steps to the front door.

At the very edge of his consciousness, somewhere out in the haze of his awareness, Jamie heard a car pulling up in the street behind him.

Jamie is in Port Barren, Hre meets Archie and waikes to archies house. And he hes a confrontation with a drunk cop.

~~Jamie goes~~ to Port

THREE

"Great!"

Parked at the curb was a dirty great F-250, with a light bar on the roof and a tarpaulin-covered lock-up cage on the rear tray. It was covered in red dust and road grime, and was so dirty that it was difficult to make out the "Police" signs on the doors. On the front was a huge bull-bar, complete with five enormous spotlights and a wired-on cow's skull.

"Shit!" This was bound to be trouble.

The front doors opened, and from the driver's side emerged one of the largest cops Jamie had ever seen — not just tall, although he must have been about six foot, but also fat. Very fat. But despite his size, the cop moved with a lithe agility that surprised Jamie. As the policeman strolled through the dirt he smiled, not a friendly welcoming smile but a tight, nasty little expression that didn't extend to his eyes. The nausea in Jamie's guts, the tension in his neck and shoulders and the spinning in his head increased still further.

"Well, you're here, eh?" For such a large man he had a surprisingly high and soft voice. "Been a while since we've had one of your type in town."

Jamie shrugged. He was pretty sure that he was about to get busted for ignoring the drunk cop, but he'd had a bit of experience with police and as a general rule they were just jumped-up city kids with a badge and a gun. If you kept your mouth shut and let them go on a bit you could usually work out what they were really like, and then deal with them more easily. This one was different — Jamie'd never come across a cop like this.

"Quiet one, eh?"

Despite his size the cop moved like lightning. With no warning his hand shot out and grabbed Jamie's throat, the grip instant and vice-like. Jamie couldn't breathe. He told himself not to struggle, not to put up a fight. Just let this bloke get it out of his system, he thought.

The fingers at his throat were long and delicate, out of proportion with the rest of the cop's body. For one insane moment, some detached part of Jamie's mind dredged up a memory of his mother, of her hands, which were slender like the cop's.

"See, the thing is," the cop continued, speaking slowly, methodically, "we don't like trouble much here in Port Barren. Don't like havin' our peace disturbed, so to speak."

His chest beginning to ache, Jamie fought the growing urge to kick out. Through blurring vision he noticed tiny details: sweat stains in the armpits of the cop's uniform, a few specks of dandruff on the shoulders, the name badge above the left chest pocket — 'Sgt E. Butcher'. The cop leaned his pudgy face down and in until Jamie could smell his breath and see the individual beads of sweat rolling down from under the brim of the wide police hat.

"There was another one like you. Problem kid from the city. Thought they'd send him up here so's he'd be our hassle and not bother all those judges and lawyers down there. All sorts of trouble he turned out to be."

Spots and small bursts of light danced across Jamie's vision.

▲ 33

"Soon as he arrived in town things started vanishing. People's property and such like. You listening to me, son?"

Jamie made a dry choking noise, trying to suck even a tiny breath of air into his burning lungs. Butcher took this as a "yes".

"I tried to talk to him, reason with him, to help him see the error of his ways. You know the sort of thing. Some of the local boys even took him aside one night and had a quiet 'chat' with him — to encourage him to behave himself. Didn't work though — that kid was trouble. Gave poor Lorraine a hell of a time, he did."

? What is that supposed to mean?

Jamie started to struggle against the suffocating grip on his throat. It was a futile effort. Butcher ignored the movement completely.

"Strange thing though — after a couple of months this kid vanished. Just like that. Guardians woke up one morning and he'd gone. Hadn't taken any food, no clothes. Nothin'. Just" — he paused for the briefest of seconds — "vanished. Very mysterious. Did a bit of a search around town but naturally no one was inclined to look too hard. Figure he must have wandered off into the desert. Never find him out there of course — desert's a big place."

Sounds like the movie/book "holes"

He released his grip and Jamie dropped onto the hard dirt. He'd never have thought that the dusty Port Barren air could taste so good. Sucking in a huge breath, he tried to clear his vision. As he crouched on his hands and knees, Butcher squatted on the ground close beside him and whispered into his ear.

"See, there's a moral to this story. A lesson. I hope you're clever enough to work it out, son, 'cause otherwise, well, you'd better be careful, watch out, that's all I'm saying."

It was the second time in ten minutes Jamie had had that warning.

Butcher walked back to the police truck. The Sergeant wasn't alone. Leaning on the passenger side was another cop, a young bloke. He wore the same khaki uniform as Butcher, but his was cleaner and cared for. The seams on the pants stood out where they had been ironed, and his hat sat squarely on his head. He must have been there the whole time, seen the entire episode, but his face was expressionless. He stared blankly at Jamie, his eyes hidden behind a pair of mirrored sunglasses. Butcher didn't seem bothered. He spoke sharply to his colleague.

— work partner (verb)

"Get in."

The young cop gave Jamie a last blank look, then turned and climbed into the passenger's seat. Before getting behind the wheel, Butcher had one last thing to say.

"Welcome to Port Barren. Stay out of trouble, eh?"

is that going to be easy for Jamie?

Jamie meets Srgent butcher and gets chored by him. Hears a story about some kid who came down in trouble and just vannished one morning. Meets another stern looking cop

Port Barren

FOUR

A dim light penetrated the dirty fly-wire screens around the verandah. Lying on his bed, Jamie looked up through the dusty mesh at the few stars bright enough to cast their glow inside. The tight feeling, the uneasiness that had filled him the moment he'd stepped off the coach a week ago was still there, resting in the pit of his stomach like a constant, nagging, weight. He hadn't had a decent night's rest since he'd arrived and tonight was no different — sleep was a long way away.

"Bugger it." He rolled off his bed and made his way to the tap on the other side of the sleep-out. His "room" was the back verandah of Archie's place, which had been walled in with fly-screens. An old fridge and a sink stood at one end and a steel-framed bed at the other. The bed was soft and comfortable.

Jamie took a chipped glass off the shelf above the sink and filled it. The pipes gave a rattle and a thump as he turned the tap. As usual the water was warm and had a faint metallic taste — during the daylight it looked cloudy.

It was two in the morning. The night air was cool. Somewhere out in the desert a dingo howled. Jamie shivered even

▲ 39

though it wasn't really cold — it was never cold in Port Barren.

He'd been to see Lorraine that afternoon. The first of his weekly check-ins. She'd been all smiles and cheerfulness.

"Jamie. How's it going? Getting along?"

He'd nodded. Grunted some short reply. In fact, when he thought about it, apart from that first run-in with Sergeant Butcher he'd been managing pretty well. Archie turned out to be easy to live with. He barely ever spoke. He might have said perhaps three words in the entire week, two of them on that first morning, after Jamie had eventually staggered inside.

Will we ever hear him speak?

He'd climbed the front steps, opened the screen door and found himself staring down a short dark passageway running through the middle of the house. After the glare of the sun outside, it had been like stepping into a cave. Even though it was probably hotter inside the house than outside, the gloom and dimness made the place feel cooler and somehow peaceful.

"Hello?"

His voice echoed down the bare hallway. In a doorway at the far end Archie's head appeared. He'd nodded and Jamie, understanding the meaning behind the gesture, had joined him in the screened-in back verandah.

"Your place." He was surprised by the old man's voice. It wasn't gravelly, weak and confused like most old people's. Archie's voice was deep and strong, with a timbre that seemed to resonate around the room. *seems like a tough guy*

"Thanks." Throwing his bag down beside the bed, Jamie sat experimentally on the mattress. "It's comfy."

Archie nodded a silent reply and went back into the house. Soon the sound of a kettle being filled floated through the screen door. Jamie unpacked his gear, taking a few minutes to get everything set up. He didn't have too much — a couple of tee-shirts, some jeans, underwear and a toothbrush. When

40 ▲

he turned again there was a cup of strong tea on the old formica-topped table by the passage door. No sign of the old man.

That set the pattern for the rest of the week. Jamie barely saw his host from day to day, and when he did, nothing was really said between them — just the odd quiet offering of a cup of tea. Jamie liked the whole set-up. It was different from what he'd expected. More importantly, it was different from what he'd experienced. There'd been no laying down of the house rules, no curfew, no sincere "I want to be your friend but only if you'll let me" talks. Nothing like the usual. The house was always peaceful and there was no pressure on him. He could come and go as he pleased — the door was never locked. *?So whats the point of this house*

That was the only thing he liked about Port Barren, though. The heat and the dust were a constant pain. Everything was always coated in a layer of pink desert sand, fine and grainy. It drifted through the town, carried by the hot breeze that blew from the south out of the Great Sandy Desert. It was into the desert that Jamie found himself staring as he sat on the back steps in the middle of the night.

There was no moon, but the light given off by the stars was enough to allow Jamie to see well away from the town. Out there were the big iron-ore mines that kept the whole region alive, but there was no sign of them from Port Barren. It was difficult to imagine the heavy machinery and burning lights out among the spiny bushes and rocky outcrops that loomed distant in the starlight. *reminds me somehow of the*

Jamie drained the glass of water. *movie "the hills have eyes"*

"No point sittin' here all night." Leaving the glass on the top step, he headed around the side of the house to the road, careful not to make any noise.

As he walked he got the feeling that something or someone was nearby, watching him. A couple of times he stopped and turned suddenly, hoping to catch whoever it was by surprise,

reminds me AGAIN of that movie.

but all he ever saw was the empty street dappled with deep, still shadows.

In the dark, Port Barren was a different place. It had the same eerie atmosphere, but the absence of light made everything seem closer, more stifling. The houses took on a dead and sinister quality. The town felt soulless. Back in the city Jamie often used to go walking at night. Sometimes he'd roamed for hours through the streets, enjoying the darkness and the shadows, trying to make himself blend in. It was different though. In the city there were still signs of life; the houses looked asleep, not dead as they did here. There were streetlights, and the occasional flickering blue glow in a window of a night owl watching late television. Kid's bikes were left in front yards, and the odd car would cruise past.

In Port Barren, apart from the clicking of the cicadas in the scrub, and the odd animal noise that drifted across from the desert, a total, unsettling stillness pervaded. The wind had dropped and the air itself was as lifeless as the darkened houses. In the city the dark had been a friend, but in Port Barren it was a different creature, full of menace and shadows and hints of movement in the corners of Jamie's vision, which vanished as soon as he looked. The longer he wandered the more uneasy he felt. The night settled upon him like a thick, suffocating blanket dropped from the sky.

He found himself by the side of the highway about a hundred metres from the admin building. The town's only street lamp threw a dirty puddle of light at the base of the front steps, and a single, naked bulb in the eaves above the admin door cast a dim glow along the verandah. Everything looked normal, quiet and dead, but the sensation that he was being watched became stronger. Hairs prickled along his arms and the back of his neck and he stood totally still.

"Stop it," he told himself. "Bloody well calm down." Some deep breaths slowed his pulse a little. He took a couple of steps towards the admin building and then stopped, a cold shiver running the length of his body.

There was a person on the verandah.

The figure stood in the shadows, out of the pool of light cast by the bare bulb. Whoever it was shifted their weight from one leg to the other. A small movement, but enough to separate one shadow from the rest. Having spotted him, Jamie could make out the person easily — a tall, slim shape, motionless. Watching.

This is weird!

He was still a little distance away, but if he ran he'd be noticed for sure. All he could do was to wait until the man on the verandah went away or looked somewhere else, and then try to fade back in the direction he'd approached from.

It seemed an eternity that the two of them stood, as still and silent as the Port Barren night, Jamie feeling hopelessly exposed in the middle of the road, and the stranger on the verandah content to remain in the shadow of an upright roof support. Jamie could feel the weight in his belly growing heavier and heavier. Sweat broke out on his forehead and he tried desperately to control his breathing, to fight down the wave of panic that threatened to swamp him.

"I should run for it." His voice was an almost silent whisper, more for reassurance than any other purpose. He could try to just creep away into the darkness, disappearing silently into the night. Or he could run. Hope that he got clear. Try to get back home. *RUN!!!*

In the end the decision was made for him. As Jamie watched, the figure came to life, searching its pockets and then placing a cigarette in its mouth. In the brief flare of the match, Jamie could make out the man's face. He drew a sharp breath. It was a face he recognised. The young cop. The expressionless one leaning against the police truck watching when Butcher had introduced himself.

"Oh shit!" The last thing he wanted was to be found by the

cops, wandering around town alone in the middle of the night. *hes an idiot*

The flare of the match died and was replaced by the tiny red pinpoint at the end of the cigarette. The cop walked slowly the length of the verandah and stepped into the glow of the light, so that he stood directly under the bulb.

This was Jamie's chance. In the light the cop would be blind to anything in the darkness outside the verandah. Jamie was edging backwards when the man took a final deep draw on the cigarette. He flicked the butt away, where it exploded on the hard ground in a miniature shower of sparks. Looking up, he exhaled the smoke; Jamie watched it curl lazily around the light bulb. The young cop stared directly into the darkness at the spot where Jamie stood. Then a tiny smile twitched at the cop's mouth and he raised his right hand in a kind of half salute — his eyes locked on Jamie.

Jamie ran. Taking flight into the shadows of Port Barren. *this should be interesting*

FIVE

"So have you met Cameron yet?"

"Who?"   ☺ trouble child

"Cameron Michaels. The other senior at school."

"Seen him around."

Lorraine's office was just as cluttered as usual. Jamie sat on the same old chair and tried to look as uninterested as possible.

"Have you been getting out much? I imagine you've had a good look around town by now."

"Not really."

Since the midnight encounter with the young cop, who's name, Jamie found out by listening to the kids at school, was Constable Robb, Jamie had been lying low. He'd fallen into the habit of heading straight back to Archie's place when school got out for the afternoon and then staying inside. For the first time in years, he was getting his homework done.

strange cop

"You should introduce yourself to Cameron. He's a nice guy, I'm sure he'd love to show you around."

Jamie had seen this Cameron kid. He was the only year twelve in the tiny, single-teacher state school. There were a couple of girls in year ten and a handful of eights and nines, but that was it for Port Barren Secondary. Less than twenty kids all up, in one classroom, with one teacher. Most of the town's kids got sent to boarding school as soon as they were old enough, or the whole family moved away when the kids reached high school. The older kids, Cameron and the year ten girls, were doing correspondence courses for most of their subjects. They were only at school a couple of days a week, to get work checked or to hand in assignments. The rest of the time they worked at home. Jamie was flat out catching up on the basics that he'd missed over the last few years. School hadn't been one of his priorities for some time.

[handwritten margin note: can't you go to bording school at any age?]

"Yeah, I might."

"You should. I think you'd like him, and you need someone to hang out with."

[handwritten margin note: might get in some trouble]

A few seconds of silence.

"How's school going?"

"Okay." Jamie would never have admitted it, but he was actually enjoying school. Without his mates to distract him he'd found it was pretty simple.

Lorraine put down the file she'd been reading, took her thick glasses off the end of her nose, and leaned back in her seat.

"You're sure there's no problems?" She had a strange expression on her face. Something was bothering her.

"Nah. No worries."

"It's just that ..."

"What?"

"I'm not sure how to put this. It's just ... well ... Sergeant Butcher came to see me the other day, over in Karratha."

"What was he doin' there?"

"He comes across from time to time, for various bits and pieces."

"So?"

"He's concerned. About you."

"Me? What for?"

She hesitated.

- Cameron could have done it

"Since you arrived there's been a few cases of vandalism about the place. He's worried that you might be involved."

"What cases?"

"Nothing major — a window broken at the back of the pub the other night, and someone's let a couple of car tyres down. That's all."

"Wasn't me."

"Jamie, Port Barren is a small place. Someone new arrives in town and suddenly there's an outbreak of vandalism, well, people notice. And talk. That's all I'm saying."

Jamie knew what she was really saying.

"This is bullshit!"

"No one's accusing you of anything. I thought you should be made aware of the situation. That's all."

"I've been home every day. And every night. Right after school. You go and ask Archie. Go on." He slammed his hand against the thin wall next to his chair. The whole building trembled. It was one thing getting busted and sent up here — it sucked, but it was fair enough. Getting accused of stuff he hadn't done was something else altogether.

they cant blane him with a townful of reckless children

"Calm down, Jamie. You're not getting blamed for any of this. I just wanted to make sure that you were warned about it, that's all. If you're staying out of the way then that's good. Keep doing it. Just don't get yourself caught out. Remember, people around here notice things and, let's face it, you don't exactly have the best record."

"How does anyone here apart from you know my record?"

Lorraine looked momentarily startled. Disconcerted. "Jamie, it's pretty clear why you're here. We've had kids sent up by the courts before, and Sergeant Butcher ..."

"Butcher's an arsehole."

"He's just doing his job ..."

"Crap. He's trying to make me look bad. I bet he did the same thing to that last kid too."

"What last kid?"

"The one that vanished."

Lorraine went very still, and leaned forward in her chair, giving him a hard look.

"How do you know about that?"

He'd made a mistake. Jamie remembered that he hadn't told Lorraine about Butcher's performance and their conversation that first day. He hadn't wanted to stir things up.

"Overheard a couple of the kids at school talking about it."

"Did you?" One of Lorraine's eyebrows twitched involuntarily. It was only a small movement but Jamie noticed it. She was still leaning right over the desk towards him, studying him closely.

not on purpose

"Yeah."

Jamie could tell she didn't believe him.

After what seemed like ages, Lorraine leaned back in her seat again. When she started speaking, she talked slowly, choosing each word carefully.

"That boy had major problems, Jamie. He was nothing like you. And when he vanished Sergeant Butcher was quite upset by the whole thing. He was in charge of organising the search, you know."

"He did a pretty average job of it."

"That's enough!" He'd never imagined Lorraine having quite that sharp tone of voice. She became more and more agitated as she spoke. "He does the best he can for this place, and he did all he could to find that boy. So don't you go making judgments about things you know nothing about. You weren't even here. They searched around this town for days. It wasn't the Sergeant's fault that they didn't find him. Sometimes people just disappear."

"Do they?"

Lorraine was still upset and ruffled, and she answered without thinking.

"Of course they do. God knows it isn't the first time around here."

oh no, they might be killing the kids.

48 ▲

"Isn't it? Who else vanished?" Jamie slipped the question in, almost catching her out again. She nearly answered straight away, but then stopped.

"What?"

"Who else disappeared round here? You just said it wasn't the first time."

"Well ... " She paused, thrown by the sudden change of subject. "The other one was different again. A couple of years earlier. There was this girl ..." ✳ This is so prising

She trailed off as she looked at her watch.

"My God! Is that the time? I'm sorry, Jamie, but I'd better get moving if I'm going to get back to Karratha this afternoon. I need to see someone there today."

"What about ..."

"I'm sorry." Lorraine was already up and out of her desk. The movement broke the mood. She was bright and cheerful, trying hard to be her usual self. Too hard, Jamie thought. "I'll be back in town next Tuesday. I don't need to see you here, but I might pop in to the school and check on how you're doing with Mr Scott."

"Yeah. Whatever."

She walked down the stairs with him. At the bottom she suddenly turned and spoke to him in a voice that was little more than a whisper.

"Jamie, be careful. You need to make a new start here, look forwards."

"Eh?"

"Don't go digging around in the past. Not here in Port Barren. Let people have their secrets."

Then she was gone.

seems like a town that has a lot of deep history.

Jamie gets accused of vandalism. he confronts Lorraine about the dissapearances. And Lorraine gets mad.

▲ 49

SIX

Jamie lay awake, tossing and turning. The disturbed feeling
still sat heavily upon him. The desert wind dropped slowly
and by half past two the night was still. A mosquito had found
its way inside and he could hear it humming in the darkness.
The air was stifling and the constant drone seemed to be
coming from right inside his skull. Once or twice he slapped
at the unseen insect, his hand striking out in the thick black
air. One time he thought he'd got it, then after a few seconds
the humming came again, relentless and annoying.

Tonight a tightness knotted his muscles, and his whole
body was tense, as though waiting for something to happen.
It was as if he was being called, drawn by an unseen force.
Jamie sat in the dark, head in his hands, trying to throw the
feeling off. Eventually he made his way silently outside to the
front of the house.

The night was still. Even the crickets, usually so constant
in their chirping, were quiet. Jamie moved cautiously through
the streets, slowly, staying deep in the shadows of the houses
and scrub, prepared to dive for cover at even the slightest
hint of movement.

There was nothing — no twitching of blinds at windows,
no flickering sensations at the corners of his vision, nothing

but stillness. Beneath his feet the hard dirt crunched gently, and he stepped lightly, keeping sound to a minimum.

He found himself at the beach. When he'd been a kid he and his brother had gone to the beach a few times. The memory of white sand and foamy crashing surf was still vivid. He had played for hours in the shallows, getting burnt to a crisp, while his brother and their mates tried to surf on an old board they'd dug up from somewhere.

The Port Barren beach was nothing like that. Jamie scrambled over sharp rocks exposed by the low tide, down onto the sand. His eyes had adapted to the faint starlight and he could see a fair bit. The sand wasn't the bright white of the beach back home; it was the same dirty red as the rest of the town, right down to the water. There was no movement, no noise. There wasn't the usual hissing of waves running onto rocks, no scraping of sand and pebbles being washed up and down, nothing. Here, the water looked like a solid, dark mirror. The ocean lay still and heavy at the edge of the sand. A different sort of desert from the one that stretched away behind Archie's house, but a desert all the same.

A little distance to the east an old wooden jetty jutted out over the sand. With the tide out, almost the entire structure stood above the waterline. A single light on a pole stood a solitary vigil at the end, its dull glow reflecting off the steely black water. Jamie headed west along the beach, away from the town. The last couple of houses fell behind, and clear of the threat of discovery he tried to relax.

He still couldn't shake the idea that something was drawing him. The sensation that he was being called along the beach was too strong to ignore. With every step it seemed to grow in urgency, until it was like a living thing, pulsing and throbbing at the centre of his brain.

About two kilometres out from the town he spotted something on the beach ahead. A large black shape crouching in darkness. He increased his pace a little, certain that this was his destination. It loomed larger and larger as he approached, slowly taking on the form of a boat.

It had a raked bow and blunt stern, a solid, box-like appearance that suggested it had been designed to do lots of hard work. It lay half on its side, propped up on a couple of old tractor tyres, well above the tide line. Sitting in the gloom on the dark sand, it seemed huge and whale-like.

He stopped a couple of metres away. One thing was obvious; this wasn't a local boat. It didn't look like any of the small fishing and recreational craft moored off the township; it was large, unwieldy and wooden. The wheelhouse was the only structure on the deck. There were no masts and no rigging.

Slowly, aware of the building tension in his body, Jamie walked around it. Even in the darkness he could see the gaping holes where planks had rotted and come away from the ribs.

The whole boat had a curiously dead feeling about it, as though it hadn't just been abandoned, but rather that it had never been alive. There was something familiar about its design, something suggestive about the sweep of the deck.

Tentatively, Jamie crept forward until he was standing right alongside the hull. His heart pounded in his ears and the night air seemed to take on a whole new thickness — he felt as though he actually had to suck it into his lungs. He reached out with his right hand, stretching towards the rough planking. His fingertips brushed against the timber.

It was like an electric shock. Spots flashed in Jamie's vision and his whole body stiffened, then he fell in a crumpled heap onto the hard red sand beside the boat.

"Hey! Wake up. You okay?"

Sunlight. Hot and blinding, dragging him back to reality.

"Huh?" Through the bright haze Jamie made out someone standing over him. The rising sun behind the figure shone a bright halo around his head and shoulders, hiding his features.

"You all right, mate?"

Jamie tried to stand but his body wouldn't let him and he slumped unsteadily back onto the dirt. *maybey the towni's posesed*

"Shit! My head." It was spinning and aching all at once.

"Had a couple, did you?"

"Eh?" It took a moment or two for Jamie to work out what the stranger meant. "Nah, nothin' like that. Just ..." He wasn't sure what had happened.

"Here, give us a hand will you?"

An outstretched hand grabbed his and yanked him easily to his feet, where he tottered unsteadily.

Jamie shook his head in an effort to clear his vision. His "rescuer" said nothing, simply watched in silence. Finally Jamie's mind started to function properly again and he looked at the other man with a flash of recognition.

"You're Cameron." *mabey cameron did that to him*

"Yeah. Jamie isn't it?"

"Yeah."

Another silence.

"I was out for my morning run when I noticed you lying here. You sure you're okay?"

"Yeah. Really, I'll be fine."

"Well we'd better get a move on then. Gotta get ready for school."

"What time is it?"

Cameron glanced at the silver sports watch on his wrist.

"Just short of seven-thirty."

"Oh man!"

"Yeah, I need to get home and shower. You look like you could do with one yourself."

The two of them started to walk towards town. Jamie cast a sideways glance at his companion. Cameron was a big guy. Not fat, muscular. He had the look of someone who did a lot of exercise — fit and in control. His sandy blond hair was messy and there were sweat stains down the back and sides of the tight blue running singlet that he wore.

After a couple of minutes Jamie stopped and looked back along the beach at the derelict boat. In the bright morning sunlight it seemed much smaller. Cameron also stopped.

reckless
or
uncontrollable

"What's up? You still okay?"

"Yeah. It's nothin'."

They continued in silence until Jamie spoke.

"Listen, don't feel like you have to walk with me or anythin'. I'll be fine. Serious."

"You sure?"

"Yeah. You finish your run. Might see you at school, eh?"

"All right." Cameron looked doubtful, but started a slow trot ahead of Jamie. He glanced back again, checking to see if Jamie was still on his feet, and then increased his pace and disappeared rapidly into the distance.

Jamie goes on a midnight stroll to the beach. He finds a mesterious looking boat. Then he is knocked out and gets wore op by cameron

SEVEN

type of animal?

It was another ten minutes before Jamie reached the outskirts of the township. He drew level with the first of the fibro bungalows and climbed up over the rocks and off the beach. It was almost eight, and the town was coming to life. A few cars whipped past, kicking up small clouds of dust as he trudged towards Archie's. It didn't matter to Jamie though, as his night on the sand had left him filthy.

He tried to remember what had happened. He'd reached out and touched the boat, then there'd been a huge flash of light and everything went black. That was all he could recall. He had a vague recollection of some strange dreams, screams and shouts and gunshots, but no matter how hard he tried to get the images to crystallise in his mind, they remained elusive.

While Jamie was lost in thought, another car cruised slowly past and pulled over to the curb ahead. He looked up — the police truck. It wasn't Butcher who climbed out of the driver's seat, though, but the young bloke, Robb. *now we get his name*

The cop retrieved his hat from the shelf behind the driver's seat, placing it carefully on his head. Then without hurrying he walked across to Jamie. As usual, his uniform was immaculate. On the thick leather belt, his pistol was buttoned firmly

▲ 55

into its holster, alongside a pair of handcuffs. He was chewing gum and wearing his mirrored glasses, hiding his eyes.

"Been looking for you." His voice was soft. Much quieter than any cop Jamie had ever dealt with.

"Why?"

"You'll see. Sarge wants a word." *more vandalism?*

"Why didn't the Sarge find me himself, then?"

"He's busy. Get in." Robb gestured towards the truck.

There wasn't a lot Jamie could do. The last thing he needed was to get the police further offside. He shrugged and walked over to the passenger's seat. Robb followed.

Neither said a word in the truck. They were heading towards admin. Jamie tried to get a closer look at his companion, without making it too obvious. He threw a quick glance sideways but all he saw was the same expressionless face staring straight ahead through the windscreen. Before they rounded the last corner Robb slowed and wound down the window, admitting a blast of warm, dusty air into the air-conditioned cabin. He spat his gum into the dirt, then raised the window again, catching Jamie's questioning expression as he did so.

"Sarge doesn't like chewing." *That makes no sence*

A small crowd of people were standing on the verandah. One was Butcher, obvious among the others because of his bulk. Jamie recognised a couple of faces from his meetings with Lorraine — people who worked in admin. The large cop detached himself from the group and strolled across to where Robb had parked.

"Jesus, Robb! What's he doing in the front? You think we put that cage on the back for the hell of it?"

The constable said nothing, his face betraying no emotion.

"What did I tell you before you left? Don't trust the little bugger. Those were my exact words. Don't trust him a bit, and what do you do? You let him ride up front where he could create all sorts of havoc. What if he'd made a grab for your gun? Eh?"

"Hang on ..." Jamie started to protest, but Butcher cut him off, poking him hard in the chest with a single finger.

"You shut your mouth. I'll get to you in a second." He turned back to the young cop. "You're an idiot sometimes, Robb. You know that? A total, bloody idiot."

"Sorry, Sarge."

"Sorry won't cut it when I'm hosing your brains out of the inside of the truck son. Don't let it happen again." *seems like they dont get along well*

"Okay, Sarge."

That seemed to be the end for Robb, at least for the moment. Butcher turned his attention to Jamie.

"Where were you last night?"

"Home."

"Bullshit. I went round there as soon as I found out what had happened here. Archie reckons you wandered off 'bout two this morning. Where'd you find him, Robb?"

The constable's voice was level and emotionless, not like someone who'd just been given a public dressing down.

"On Michaelson Street. Over near the beach."

"Long way from Archie's. What were you up to over there?"

"Nothin'. I couldn't sleep, so I went for a walk."

"Did you now?"

"Yeah."

Butcher didn't comment. He gave Jamie a long, slow look up and down.

"How'd you get so dirty?" *he should tell Sarge the story*

"Fell asleep on the sand." There was no point lying, and besides, Jamie couldn't think of a better excuse.

"On the sand? Why not at home in your own bed, eh?"

Jamie stayed mute. He wasn't happy with the direction that this conversation was heading. Butcher grabbed his arm.

"Come here."

He turned abruptly and walked across to the verandah, dragging Jamie in his wake. Jamie had only a second to cast a quick glance towards Robb, who was staring at something further up the highway. As he climbed the steps he could feel the eyes of the ten or fifteen people standing there following his every move. He smiled at the ones he knew, but no one smiled back.

"What do you say to that, then?" Butcher shoved him forward along the verandah a little.

"What?"

"Don't be clever with me, son. The windows." There was menace in Butcher's voice.

*it honesty ould have been Jamie; sleepwalking

Every window in both the admin building and the mining company office was smashed. There were shards of glass all over the place. Someone had swept out an area in front of the door, which was where everyone had gathered, but the rest of the verandah was covered with broken slivers glinting like diamonds in the morning sun.

"Well?"

"Well what?"

"So where'd you get to last night? And don't give me that bullshit about going for a walk."

His mind went blank. He could see exactly what Butcher was suggesting. Could feel the animosity radiating towards him from the crowd of people listening to every word. He wanted to protest, to defend himself, but he couldn't come up with a coherent thought. In the end he simply told the truth.

~ what does that mean?

"It wasn't me."

Someone in the crowd gave a brief snort and there was murmuring. Jamie heard one voice swear. Butcher smiled — a glittering snake smile that twitched at the corners of his mouth. One eyebrow climbed almost imperceptibly above the other. He reached out and Jamie readied himself for a blow, but to his surprise the long, slender fingers simply came to rest lightly on his shoulder. Even through his tee-shirt, Jamie could feel the clamminess of the policeman's hand.

"Listen son, we all know you've had a hard time settling in and everything. Everyone here has heard about your little adventures back in the city. How about you just own up and we'll get all this settled, eh? Don't make any more trouble. How about it?"

Jamie knew what he was being asked to do.

"But ..."

Both the smile and the friendly hand vanished. Now Butcher gripped his shoulder, his fingers digging hard into the soft flesh. He turned his head slightly.

"Robb!"

The constable, who'd moved up onto the verandah, stepped forward.

"Yeah, Sarge?"

"Put him in the truck. The back this time."

Robb didn't reply. Jamie started to protest.

"Hang on ..."

"No, you hang on, son," interrupted Butcher. "I warned you when you got here to stay out of trouble. Not to piss anyone off. I thought I made my message pretty clear. Seems you're a bit too thick to understand a friendly warning, though. You're going back to the city and off to remand. God help me, I'll see that happen even if I have to drive you to the prison gates myself. Put him in the truck, Robb."

Robb took Jamie's arm.

"Come on."

Deciding that for now he'd better just stay quiet and do as he was told, Jamie followed. Pulling a set of keys from his pocket, Robb unlocked the mesh gate of the lock-up cage.

"Mind your head."

The cage was bare and dirty. There was nothing to sit on, just the steel floor. The door swung closed behind him with a solid clunk as the lock was driven home, and Jamie sank

he should stay

* They dont have any proof

▲ 59

into a blue gloom as the morning sunlight penetrated the dirty tarpaulin cover. It was roasting hot. The truck was parked in direct sunlight and the covers kept any fresh air or breeze out of the cage; it was like being in an oven. Within seconds he was sweating rivers. Wide corrugated ridges ran the length of the metal floor, making it even less comfortable to sit on.

It must have been at least fifteen minutes before Jamie heard voices coming towards him, and the front doors being opened and slammed. The engine started and the truck got under way. In the back, Jamie bounced around. There were no decent handholds and everything was slippery with dust. Each time the truck rounded a corner he tried to brace himself, but there was usually no warning, no way to tell which direction they were going to turn. Whoever was driving was taking the corners late and fast. The suspension was hard and Jamie felt every bump and corrugation in the road through the steel floor.

It should have been only about two or three minutes to the police station, but they seemed to drive around for ages. The only relief was that the movement of the vehicle caused the tarpaulin covers to flap, moving some of the hot air around inside the cage.

When they eventually pulled up, Jamie breathed a sigh of relief and readied himself to climb out. The cage didn't open. Nobody came around to the back of the vehicle. Instead, Butcher's disembodied voice floated in through the canvas.

"Afraid we've only got the one lock-up cell here, and Constable McPhearson's sleeping off a hangover in there at the moment. Wouldn't want to wake up a member of the force now, would we? You'll have to wait out here for a bit. If you want anything, just give us a shout."

He laughed, and Jamie heard the crunch of footsteps retreating across gravel.

"Hey!" He yelled a couple of times, but Butcher and Robb had disappeared.

The temperature climbed steadily. The rising sun heated the steel of the chassis, and in the cage Jamie cooked. His mouth was dry and he could feel his lips cracking. After an hour the first pangs of hunger gripped his stomach. Calling did no good — there was no response. Eventually, he stretched out on the hot, uneven steel floor.

He began to drift in and out of consciousness as his thirst became more and more intense. He closed his eyes, tried to retreat into darkness, but found himself swimming in a blur of movement. A sudden, overpowering presence invaded him, swamping his mind with panic and fear. It was the feeling of Port Barren amplified a thousand times. He thought he heard a girl's voice. It seemed to be coming from somewhere outside, but then as he sat up and looked around something seemed to shift, the air itself moved about him and the voice was inside the cage. He tried to reply, tried to speak back, but his voice refused to work. He didn't understand what she was saying. He thought that his mind was playing tricks on him, and he concentrated on the words, but they remained elusive. Strange words in another language.

A minute seemed like an hour, and an hour like a second. Without his watch Jamie had no way of knowing exactly how long he had been trapped, but the longer he was locked up the more insistent became the feeling that someone was in there with him. At one point, waking from a spell of thirst-induced unconsciousness, he was convinced that he'd felt a hand touch his cheek. But as his vision cleared there was no one there — nothing but dim, blue light seeping through the tarpaulin.

Eventually he couldn't take it any more. Jamie began to yell and scream, striking at the steel mesh of the cage with his fist again and again until a trickle of blood ran from his knuckles. He sucked at it, the salt taste running down the

▲ 61

back of his throat, making his thirst even more fierce. Finally, mercifully, he passed out once more, this time into a deep sleep.

"Get him out of there!"

"Hurry up, Robb."

"I can't believe you, Butcher! How could you do this to him? Don't you ever learn?"

"Calm down, Lorraine, he'll live."

"He'd better. I'm telling you, if anything happens to this one ..."

"Are you threatening me, Lorraine?"

"No. Not at all. It's just not like last time. Remember that."

"I'd say you're the one who needs to do some remembering ..."

Voices. Like sounds from a great distance away, floating down to where Jamie slept. Then a coolness, trickling against his skin, over his eyes. A sensation of being lifted, carried, then finally, total sleep.

They DID kill the other kids

Jamie getts picked op by robb, Jamie is accused of vandalism on the admin house. And sargent butcher leavs him in a realhy hot truck, so he has a little heat stroke.

EIGHT

Jamie woke. The first thing he became aware of was the smell, clean and antiseptic. The light was blinding — a harsh, fluorescent white glare that seared the backs of his eyes. Slowly the brightness resolved itself into a white ceiling. It was cool — air-conditioned. He tried to sit up.

"Steady." Lorraine was sitting a metre away on a tall-backed nursing chair.

meter?

"What hap —"

The bile rose in his throat, and Jamie rolled himself sidways, vomiting onto the floor next to the bed.

"Shit!"

The doctor, who'd been standing in the shadows, stepped forward.

"It's okay. Just lie down and relax."

He rested his hand briefly on Jamie's forehead, then looked at Lorraine.

"Still a little high. Not to worry though, it's coming down." Glancing at the mess on the floor his nose wrinkled in distaste. "I'll find a mop and a bucket and clean this up."

Lorraine stood up.

"No, you'd better stay here with him. I'll do it. Where do I look?"

The doctor shrugged.

"Try the utility cupboard at the end of the hall. I think that's where they keep the cleaning gear."

Lorraine walked from the room, and the doctor, taking no further interest in his patient, sat down in the chair she'd just vacated, pulled a novel from his pocket, and started leafing through the pages. Jamie used the opportunity to try to work out where he was.

It was sort of like a hospital room, but not really. He was lying in the only bed, made up with striped blue and white sheets, the initials GNMC stitched into the top corner near his shoulder. A drip ran into his arm, with a clear solution trickling slowly from the bag down the feeder tube.

Lorraine returned, mop and bucket in hand, and busied herself alongside the bed.

"Where am I?" His voice sounded gravelly and scratchy. Strange, even to his own ears. Lorraine put the mop down and fetched him a glass of water from a sink over near the wall.

"Here."

"Thanks." He sipped at it, the coppery taste tricking slowly down the back of his throat and settling in his stomach. It felt like there was sand under his eyelids.

"You're in the mining company nursing station. You know, the small prefab behind admin?"

"What time is it?"

"Six-thirty in the evening. You've been asleep all afternoon."

"What happened?"

"I went around to the school to see you. Mr Scott told me you weren't there, so I went to let Sergeant Butcher know. He told me about the windows."

The windows. He'd forgotten about them. The memory of the shattered shards glinting in the morning sunlight came back to Jamie like a sick weight in the pit of his guts.

"I didn't do it."

"We'll talk about it later. When you're feeling better."

Jamie grabbed her arm. *he should tell lorraine what happened*

"I didn't do it."

Silence hung between them for a couple of seconds. The doctor coughed. Eventually Lorraine answered.

"That's not what the Sergeant said."

"He's full of it. I told him where I was last night."

"He doesn't believe you."

"Do you?"

Again, silence was her answer. It was obvious what she thought.

"If I'm so guilty, then why am I here and not in the lock-up?"

"The state you were in when I found you, Jamie, this was the only place for you. Besides, I don't care what Sergeant Butcher thinks of you; there's no excuse for treating anyone the way he treated you this morning."

"I could do him for that."

"What do you mean?"

"You know, report him. Officially."

"You could try." There was skepticism in her voice. *unsure or not clear*

"You don't reckon I'd get him?"

"With your history? No, I don't. Anyway, he's got an excuse. That drunk McPherson was already locked up. The Sergeant will just say that he made a mistake and didn't realise what condition you were in. No one will take your word over his, Jamie."

"That's crap."

"It's the way things are."

"What happens now then?"

"What do you mean?"

"You know. 'Bout the windows and that."

Lorraine sat forward on her chair. An expression of surprise flickered across her face.

"Are you admitting that you did it?"

"No. But it looks like Butcher's pretty much got it in for me, and there's not much I can do about it, is there? I'm stuffed."

"Don't jump to conclusions."

"Eh?"

Lorraine was quiet again. When she spoke again, her voice was different — careful, more cautious.

"Jamie, when we hauled you out of the truck, do you remember what you were saying?"

Jamie's brow furrowed with concentration. A few shadowy recollections formed in his head — the heat and the thirst, and some vague idea of a girl speaking to him — but he couldn't form any clear pictures or memories.

"Nah. It's all a blur."

"You kept talking about a boat. And a girl." *thats like what his episode was abt*

"Did I?" He strained again to remember, but the memories still refused to reveal themselves. *he touched that boat*

"I can't remember anythin' about that."

"Well you were. You were saying all sorts of strange things."

"Like what?"

"Nothing that made any sense — just bits and pieces. About being trapped and locked up, about hiding, bullets, darkness."

"What's that got to do with the windows?"

The question caught her by surprise. She answered quickly. Too quickly.

"Nothing. It was just strange, that's all." She stopped, aware of how lame her response was "I thought you might have been remembering something from one of your foster homes. It sounded pretty nasty, and I was worried. That's all."

Jamie wondered why Lorraine was going on about it.

"You still haven't told me why they let you get me out."

"You've got an alibi."

"Eh?" *Cameron saw him!*

66 ▲

"Not a very strong one, but enough to give me a bit of leverage with Sergeant Butcher on your behalf."

"Who?"

"Cameron." *i was right*

"Cameron?" It took a few seconds for the name to register. "The big kid from school?"

"That's the one. News travels fast around here. When you didn't show up for school and he heard that you'd been arrested, he came down to the station and told us how and where he'd found you this morning. Said you looked pretty messed up."

"So?"

"Well at least it tied in with your story about going for a walk. I managed to convince Sergeant Butcher that if you were passed out so far away from the town, then it was possible that you hadn't been responsible for the vandalism. Added to that was the way he treated you this morning. If there's a chance that you were already ill — and from what Cameron told us you weren't in very good nick — then he had no right to act the way he did." *her thats my name*

"You scared him?" Jamie looked at Lorraine with a sort of respect.

"Let's just say I pointed out a couple of truths to him. I don't think he'll want to risk making a fuss about this. It mightn't look too good on his career record."

Jamie took another sip of his water. Suddenly he felt tired. Very tired. All he wanted to do was sleep for about three weeks.

"But Jamie, this doesn't mean you're out of the woods, not by a long shot. The Sergeant is still firmly convinced that you're the culprit and he's going to move heaven and hell to get you out of Port Barren. You can't afford even the slightest slip-up. Right now, he'd probably try to get you put into remand for littering."

Lorraine's words barely registered. As Jamie battled the

sudden waves of fatigue that swept over him, her voice seemed to come from far away.

"I'll be careful."

"You'd better be, because you were lucky this time. Very lucky. You owe Cameron a big thank-you."

"Yeah." Even his own voice sounded detached. Lorraine noticed how tired he was getting.

"I'll let you sleep. The doctor will be nearby if you need anything."

She got up to leave but turned back at the door.

"Jamie?"

"Yeah?" He could feel his last grip on consciousness fading.

"Be very careful."

"I will."

He fell asleep, dropping into unconsciousness as though into a thick and comfortable mattress. *sounds like me right now* *what does that mean*

In his dreams the walls of the nursing station seemed to be closing in. Slowly, inexorably. The harsh white light of the fluorescent tubes on the ceiling grew brighter and brighter — invading, penetrating his thoughts, washing away his being in a sea of white coolness. There was a sound — a *sounds like a shipwreck* gentle, quiet, desperate whimpering. There were voices, male, deep and harsh, arguing and shouting, floating in and out of his hearing, as though washed by an invisible tide. Then there were hands — lifting, pulling, grabbing. Dragging him from the soft coolness out into the night. Into the heat and dust. Into a steel cage. Into darkness.

Jamie woke with a scream. The blue and white blankets and sheets of the bed were soaked through with the sweat that poured off him. The blankets were wrapped around his arms and legs. Tangling, suffocating. He struggled to free himself, caught in the netherworld between consciousness and sleep. The nightmare still had a hold on him, but the *non-existant world?*

reality of where he actually was slowly seeped into his understanding.

A sharp pain at his elbow snapped him fully into wakefulness. The doctor was standing over his bed.

"Are you all right? You pulled your drip out."

He adjusted the small tappet on the plastic hose, and the
clear fluid began to flow again.

"Would you like a sedative? You must have been dreaming."

Jamie shook his head, sinking back against the pillow,
rearranging the sheets. The doctor took his temperature
again.

"It's still coming down. You'll feel better in the morning."

As the man left the room, he flicked the lights off. Lying
awake in the sudden darkness, the shapes of the fluorescent
tubes burned an imprint into Jamie's eyes.

Jamie wakes up in the
hospital. He gets an
alibi from cameron on
whare he was the night
of the vandalism. And
he has a very horifying
dream,

NINE

"Hey!"

Cameron stopped at the shout, glancing back to where Jamie approached from the other side of the playground. He said something to the two year-ten girls he'd been walking with. One threw him a strange look, then the two of them continued on their own towards the classroom, chatting as they went. Cameron waited as Jamie walked gingerly across the dirt schoolyard. Even now, three days after his night in the nursing station, he still felt a little light-headed.

"Uhm, thanks for the other day and everything."

Jamie kept his eyes on the ground and tried to look as bored and disinterested as possible. The other kids were watching them from the school verandah. He knew they'd heard stories about him, and he'd deliberately stayed away from them. Still, after what Cameron had done for him, he knew he at least had to say thanks.

"That's okay. How're you feeling?" There was something a little distant about the other boy's manner.

"All right."

The conversation lapsed into awkward silence, Jamie staring intently at something in the dirt and Cameron shifting his weight restlessly from one foot to the other. They were saved from their discomfort by the school bell. As its raucous jangle faded, Cameron spoke.

"We'd better get inside."

"Yeah."

Cameron started towards the verandah. He'd only managed a step or two when Jamie grabbed his arm, his grip strong and insistent. Turning, Cameron found himself staring directly into Jamie's eyes. For a couple of seconds they stood motionless, their stares locked. It was Jamie who finally spoke.

"I didn't do it."

"The windows?"

Jamie nodded. Cameron raised an eyebrow.

"Then who did?" Shaking his arm free of Jamie's grip, Cameron walked up the stairs into the classroom.

Alone in the dusty playground, Jamie watched Cameron's receding figure, trying to work out why it was so important that Cameron believe him. No answer presented itself and in the end all he could do was go to class.

"Stuff it!" He grabbed his schoolbag and followed the last of the younger kids inside.

All day Jamie felt unfocussed. Sitting in his usual seat at the back, he copied notes off the board and opened his books up on all the right pages, but his gaze kept drifting to where Cameron sat, his large frame crammed behind a desk a couple of rows up ahead. At one point Mr Scott wandered over.

"Jamie, everything okay?"

Jamie nodded. The teacher lowered his voice and crouched, balancing on his haunches.

"Lorraine told me about the other day. Don't look angry, she has to — it's her job. If there's any problems, any worries, you let me know, okay?"

Jamie grunted a reply that might have been an affirmative.

"Now, you sure you're all right?"

"Yeah."

"Well, tell me if you start feeling off-colour. You can take the afternoon to rest if you need to. You've been through a bit of an ordeal and I'd hate to see it get in the way of your schoolwork. I need you back on task, mate."

The teacher stood and moved down the row. Jamie tried to start his math X but the numbers refused to go together. Again and again his thoughts returned to the old wreck on the beach, to the heat and the thirst in the cage of the police truck. Always in the background was the voice. Soft, feminine and undecipherable. First in the truck, and then later, whimpering, in the hospital. Eventually he gave up trying to do geometry and let his mind wander.

Cannot crack the code/language

By lunchtime Jamie hadn't done any more work. Packing up, he was surprised to find his page covered with scribble. Doodles and drawings — he must have been doing them while he day-dreamed. Not surprisingly, the boat was there in the middle of the page, propped on its old tractor tyres. In one corner was the police truck, a hand poking out from between the bars. There were other things too — patterns and pictures he couldn't identify. A lot of them were nothing more than strange swirls on the stark white paper, curves of pencil bisecting the rigid lines of the exercise book.

There was a buzzing in his head and his vision was blurring. Gathering his books, he walked up to Mr Scott's desk at the front of the classroom. *Jamie needs to see*

"Jamie?"

Some Professional

"I'm not feelin' too flash. I might take the afternoon off to sleep if that's okay?"

The teacher sat back in his chair and surveyed Jamie thoughtfully, chewing on the end of a pencil.

"No worries. The other seniors are all home this afternoon anyway for correspondence classes, so it won't be a problem. You go and rest and I'll see you tomorrow."

As Jamie turned, the teacher's voice stopped him;

"Jamie —"

Jamie glanced back.

"I'm pretty impressed with the way you've applied yourself so far. I just thought you should know that."

Jamie nodded and left the classroom.

Outside, with the hot desert wind blowing dry, red dust into his face, Jamie turned towards Archie's. He couldn't get rid of the thickness that seemed to be enveloping his thoughts, as though his head had somehow become detached from the rest of him. He caught himself staggering slightly, and leaned against a low wall to catch his breath.

"Shit. What's goin' on?"

He slumped against the wall and something grabbed at him, pulling him back along the road, away from Archie's place. It took a few seconds to work out what was happening. Like the other evening, his feet had taken on a life of their own, drawing him back past the school. Through a bewildered haze he realised that he was going back to the beach, returning to the boat.

The further he walked the less intense the fog in his head became. By the time he reached the beach and climbed down the rocks he felt almost like his old self again, only the familiar tightness in the pit of his belly to remind him that he was still in Port Barren.

In daylight, the wrecked boat didn't appear nearly as large or foreboding. It was nothing more than a decaying hulk, dumped on some old tyres on the sand. As he came nearer Jamie felt some of the tension lift from his shoulders and neck and he began to experience a sense of calm detachment. Walking along the beach, watching the black shape shimmer in the heat haze, an inexplicable sense of relief washed over him.

The harsh elements of the north-west had bleached and pitted the wood of the vessel, leaving it pale and fragile. It reminded Jamie of the skeleton of a decaying beast — a beached whale perhaps, delicate and yet still suggesting the power of its former self. A strange and frightening beauty.

Reaching out to touch the wooden hull, Jamie hesitated, remembering the burst of light and pain he'd experienced when his fingertips last made contact with the boat. Taking a deep breath, he rested the palm of his hand gently against the wood. This time there was no flash, no unconsciousness. The wood felt rough and strangely cool in the midday sun. Trailing his hand gently across the surface, wary of splinters, he made a slow circut.

On the far side a section of the railing around the deck had crumbled and a couple of exposed planks made it possible to climb up and get on board. Carefully, Jamie eased his weight onto one of the ribs, unsure whether it would support him. It creaked a little but it held and Jamie swung himself up onto the deck.

It was rotten and treacherous. Planks were missing, with splinters driving up here and there. There were sections where the timber had decayed completely and fallen down into the hold. Slowly Jamie picked his way towards the wheelhouse, stepping only on the places where he could see the planks firmly attached to the support beams beneath, places where the decking was properly nailed down. The whole structure felt as though it might fall apart beneath him at any second. In front of the wheelhouse gaped a hatchway, the remains of a wooden ladder leading down into darkness. Without stopping to consider his actions, Jamie swung his legs over and eased himself gently into the hold, using the edges of the hatch for support.

He had to walk crouched over, as the roof was too low for him to stand up straight. Sunlight streamed through gaps in the hull, lancing the gloomy air with laser-like intensity. The places where the upper deck had fallen through were silver slits in the roof, the bright midday sun throwing small, intense, uneven patches of light onto the wooden floor. In the light-beams, Jamie could see dust particles drifting lazily in the still air.

Inside, the timbers weren't quite so badly decayed, perhaps thanks to the protection of the hull. Even so there were still holes underfoot, some of them large, so Jamie explored cautiously.

He listened with cat-like concentration, expecting at any time to hear the creak of the deck giving way beneath his weight. Once, as he crept onto a new section of decking, he froze as the planks beneath him flexed and moaned a quiet protest at the unexpected load. As he crouched, dead still, barely daring to breathe, he thought he heard a noise from outside. A couple of seconds convinced him that his ears were playing tricks. He eased himself onto all fours — it would be easier to crawl. His stomach filled with an empty hollow feeling and his head spun. He stopped still.

As he waited for the dizziness to pass, a sound reverberated ominously through the dusty interior of the boat. It set Jamie's heart hammering against the inside of his chest, so that he could hear it pounding in his ears. The faint scrape of a boot against the hull. The noise seemed to echo through the long silence that followed it. Someone was coming aboard.

was halucinating

Jamie goes to school in a funk. And goes to the Boat. Finds someone there too

The Boat

TEN

Panicked, Jamie looked around. There was no way to get off the boat. For a second or two he toyed with the idea of trying to smash his way out through the rotting planks on the side of the hull, but there was no point. Even if he managed it, he'd be heard, spotted and caught before he could set foot on the beach. He had no cover and no options. All he could do was hide.

Footsteps echoed on the deck above. Whoever it was, they weren't walking carefully. Either they knew their way around the boat or didn't realise how badly the timbers had decayed. Jamie's mind raced. His breathing floated back to him, as though it was being broadcast through an amplifier. Crawling quietly forward, he approached a large gap in the floorboards. The deck had crumbled, leaving an opening straight down into the dark bilges. Easing himself into the blackness, Jamie tried to ignore the fact that the hole looked like a gaping mouth. The hull was too deep for him to reach the bottom with his feet. He paused for a second, unsure whether or not to risk dropping into the unknown. In the end the choice was made for him. The footsteps above stopped. His pursuer had reached the upper hatchway. A pair of legs appeared in the puddle of light at the far end of the deck.

Taking a deep breath Jamie dropped into the bottom of the boat. Luckily, it was filled with sand, which cushioned his fall slightly. Rolling a little, he came up against the side of the hull where he eased himself slowly, silently, into a sitting position, his back hard up against the timbers.

He was trapped in a tiny space only a couple of metres wide. The walls angled inwards to where they met in the deep V of the keel buried beneath his feet. Dim light filtered down from above, the brightest spot being under the hole through which Jamie had just dropped. He inched away from the pool of light, seeking protection in the deep shadows along the sides.

Above him, the footsteps creaked their way forward, moving inevitably towards the hole in the deck. Towards his only escape route. The air was hot and dry and he'd stirred up a lot of dust. Jamie felt the beginnings of a sneeze start to tickle at the back of his throat. He grabbed his nose and held his breath, until, with agonising slowness, the sensation subsided.

From nowhere he heard the voice. The girl's voice. It floated unbidden into his mind, her soft even tones ringing in his ears. Closing his eyes, Jamie was somewhere else. Gunshots, screaming, laughter and the voice, always there, soft and scared, speaking strange words. Before he was able to work out what was happening, without any warning he sneezed.

In the stillness the sound rang like an explosion. The footsteps stopped dead, almost directly above his head.

Silence. Deadly, total silence. In the dusty darkness Jamie held his breath. A board creaked as the person above shifted their weight.

Another slow groan. Then a crack — a gunshot. No, not a gunshot, but timber. Dry, brittle timber splintering and cracking and giving way. A figure crashed through the deck and thudded heavily onto the sand, right by Jamie's feet.

Jamie dived for the shape in the darkness, his hand already

balling into a fist. He knew from years of fighting in play-grounds and on the streets that he had to catch whoever it was by surprise. His arm swung, building momentum until it buried itself deep in the belly of his opponent. The air exploded from the man in a hot burst, right by Jamie's ear. As the man tried without success to straighten up, Jamie realised how big his opponent was. Taking a step backwards he readied himself to launch his next punch, giving himself room to push whatever slight advantage his surprise attack had given him. Before he could throw his fist through the dark-ness, however, the figure spoke.

"Jamie! Hang on."

The surprise of hearing his name stopped Jamie's arm mid-swing. He strained his eyes, trying to identify the person doubled over at his feet. Whoever it was took a minute or two to stand upright. A beam of light fell across his features.

"Cameron?"

"Yeah." Although still winded, the other boy managed a lopsided grin. "Bloody hell, mate, I thought you were going to kill me."

"I was. You scared the shit out of me."

"Sorry."

"Don't apologise. I shouldn't have hit you. You all right?"

"I'll live."

They looked at each other, both shaking and covered in dirt and sand. Jamie peered through the gloom.

"Mate, I can't see too well down here but you look like you've just gone ten rounds with a heavyweight champion."

"Don't flatter yourself. Anyway, wait till you get to a mirror."

Cameron started to laugh. At first Jamie looked at him as though he'd gone mad, but it was infectious and Jamie felt the corners of his mouth start to twitch. The two of them collapsed on the sand in the bottom of the boat, tears running down their cheeks. It took two or three minutes of solid laughter before they were able to compose themselves again.

"Man, that felt great."

"Yeah. Does you good, doesn't it?"

"Haven't had a laugh like that in a while."

"Well, you haven't had a lot to laugh about, have you?"

"Eh?"

"With everyone being warned off you and all that."

The last traces of mirth died. Jamie looked at Cameron.

"What do you mean?"

"By Butcher ..." Cameron's voice trailed off. "You haven't heard about it?"

"I heard there were a few bullshit stories about me floatin' around the place. What's this about being warned off?"

The large boy looked uncomfortable.

"A couple of days after you arrived in town, Butcher came round to the school one afternoon. It must have been a day or two before you started coming to classes. He took the seniors aside, me and the two girls, and told us to steer clear of you. Said you were trouble and that it was up to us to make sure that the word got out among the kids to give you a wide berth."

"He tell you why I was sent up here?"

"Told us you stole cars and robbed a couple of liquor stores."

"That's bullshit."

"Is it?"

" 'Course it is. They don't put you in isolated care for armed robbery. I oughta know."

"Why?"

" 'Cause my brother ..." Jamie stopped, aware all of a sudden that he barely knew this guy.

"Your brother ..." Cameron prompted.

Jamie hesitated.

"This is between you and me, right?"

"What is?"

"What I'm about to tell you. Don't spread it around, okay? There's enough rubbish about me already goin' around this town. No point adding the truth to it, is there?"

"Yeah, sure. Okay."

Still Jamie hesitated, reluctant to reveal his background. He couldn't see any way out of it, though.

"Eddie, my brother, he's banged up at the moment. For robbery."

Cameron went very quiet.

"Sorry."

"Nah, it's all right. Not your fault. Not like scaring the hell out of me back then."

The mood lightened again. They both leaned against the sides of the boat, relaxing.

"What about your folks?"

"My mum's dead. Died when I was a little tacker."

"And your dad?"

Jamie shrugged. "Who knows? He shot through a couple of years after Mum died. We hear from him every now and again, but it's mostly just me and Eddie." A thought occurred to him. " What are you doing out here anyway?"

Even in the dark, it was obvious that Cameron looked embarrased.

"I saw you leaving town. You walked right past our place and I noticed you were headed back towards the beach. I figured you might be heading here again, so I decided to follow you."

"Why?"

A slight hesitation.

"No reason really. It's just that after the other night and everything I thought ..."

He stopped.

"What?"

"I thought you mighta been doing drugs, or drinking out here or something. I was curious."

Jamie looked away. The knot in his stomach had almost vanished during the last few minutes, but now it returned, tighter than ever.

"I don't do that sort of stuff, okay?"

"Yeah. Sorry. I realise that now, it was just that after what Butcher told us ..."

Jamie grabbed his arm, tightly. He looked straight at Cameron. Even through the gloom the other boy could see the burning deep inside Jamie's eyes.

"Don't judge me by what that arsehole says. He doesn't know anything about me, and neither do you."

Another long silence. The tension hung between them, almost a tangible force in the close atmosphere. In the end it was Cameron who diffused the situation.

"I'm sorry. Really."

Jamie let go and turned away.

"Whatever."

Cameron reached out, resting his hand lightly on the other boy's shoulder. Jamie was tense, like a coiled spring ready to unwind.

"You okay?"

"Yeah. Just a bit strung out. That's all. This place gets to me."

"I know what you mean. You get used to it, though."

"Eh?"

"The uneasiness — the feeling. Everyone here experiences it. All the kids anyway. After you've been here a while you get a bit more used to it. It becomes part of the background."

Jamie stared.

"What're you talkin' about?"

"You know, Port Barren. That weird feeling you get here, like you're all screwed up inside the whole time. Don't tell me you haven't noticed it? Everyone does, especially when they're new."

Jamie's mind raced.

"You mean it's not just me?"

"No way. The first year or so after my old man moved us up here I could barely concentrate on anything. That's why I took up running. Helps me clear my mind, getting away from the town. I wouldn't normally stop out here, though."

"Out here?"

"At the boat."

"Why not?"

"Dunno really, it's just ..." he stopped.

"What?"

"You won't laugh?"

"'Bout what?"

Cameron stayed silent. It seemed as though this time it was him weighing up what he knew about Jamie, making a decision about him.

"It's probably just a kid's story." Behind his words, a note of hesitation revealed itself.

"What is?"

" 'Bout this boat."

"What about it?"

Cameron didn't get a chance to answer.

"Listen —"

In the gloomy silence Jamie heard it — the sound of an engine approaching along the beach. Coming towards the boat.

ELEVEN

"What is it?"

"Who is it, more likely."

The two boys stared at each other. Cameron shook his head, clearly puzzled.

"No one ever comes out this way. There's nothing here apart from this wreck."

"Give us a leg up to the top deck. We'll find a hole and take a look out, eh?"

Hooking his fingers together into a stirrup, Cameron hoisted Jamie through the hole in the roof, then hauled himself up as well. Jamie crawled across to the other side of the hull and found a suitable peephole.

"Oh, shit!"

"What?" Cameron dropped down beside him.

"Butcher!"

The outline of the approaching police truck was clear. The lights on the roof glinted in the midday sun, even through the shimmering haze off the sand. About four or five hundred metres away it slowed down.

"What do you think he's doin' out here?"

Cameron shrugged. "No idea."

"We'd better get out."

"And go where? As soon as we hit the beach he'll see us. The tree line's too far away to get to. I could probably talk my way out of it, find an excuse for being here, you know, but you ..."

He didn't need to finish. Lorraine's words rang in Jamie's mind: "Right now, he'd probably try to get you put into remand for littering." Given that he'd been let out of school in order to go home and sleep, Jamie guessed that truancy would serve Butcher's purpose equally as well.

"What do we do then?" demanded Jamie.

"Let's sit tight."

"What!"

"Think about it. Butcher must weigh at least a hundred and twenty kilos. No way is he going to try getting on board. This thing'd fall apart under him. As I see it, our best option is to stay put and see what happens."

Jamie wasn't happy, but they were out of alternatives. He turned his attention back to the peephole.

The four-wheel drive stopped only a few metres from where they were crouching. Butcher and Robb climbed out. Reaching back into the cab, the sergeant pulled his night-stick from behind the driver's seat.

"I don't like the look of this." Jamie's voice was little more than a hoarse whisper, barely louder than the volume of his breathing.

"What?" asked Cameron. "Give us a look."

Jamie slid aside and Cameron dropped his eye to the hole. For a few seconds he peered intently, then abruptly pulled away. Jamie bent his head towards the hole again, but Cameron restrained him, putting his finger to his lips and shaking his head.

Two sets of footsteps came directly towards where they were hiding and stopped almost beside them. Even through the timber the conversation rang loud and clear.

"Keep your eyes open, Robb."

"What for, Sarge?"

"Anythin'. Just have a look around."

"It'd help if you told me exactly what we're looking for. I still don't know why I had to come out here anyway. It's McPherson's shift."

There was the sound of a cigarette lighter scraping into life.

"Put that bloody thing out, you moron!" Butcher spat the words. "I swear, Robb, sometimes I don't know how you even passed the entrance tests. And as for McPherson, I'm in charge around here, and I'll decide who does what. If I wanted that drunken bugger out here then I'd bring him, but I don't, so you'll have to do."

They moved away and their voices became muffled. After a slow circuit of the hull, the two policemen returned to their original position.

"He was here all right. There's footprints everywhere."

"Why's it so important, anyway?"

Silence. When Butcher spoke again his voice was soft and menacing. It was the same tone he'd used that first afternoon outside Archie's place.

"Robb, I've told you a hundred times, don't ask questions about things that don't concern you."

"But —"

"Enough! One of these days you're gonna stick your nose too far into someone else's business and get it punched."

The threat behind the words was clear. Robb went very quiet. After a couple of minutes Butcher spoke again.

"Get your torch from the truck. Have a look on board."

This time the only reply was the sound of the young cop's footsteps crunching across the beach away from the boat. Jamie turned to Cameron, horrified, but Cameron was already crawling back over to the hole down into the bilges. Following, Jamie noticed the fresh marks in the dust and the jagged splinters of timber poking up at strange angles where

Cameron had fallen through earlier. No way would Robb miss the hole, assuming he got inside.

Cameron was already lowering himself silently onto the sand in the bottom of the wreck. With his extra height, he was just able to reach, and he silently eased himself down into the dark. Jamie hesitated, until the sound of Robb's footsteps returning propelled him into action.

Dropping awkwardly, he felt his knee wrench as he hit the sand. He gasped as pain shot up his leg. Cameron scurried across.

"You okay?" Just the barest of whispers. Jamie nodded, trying to ignore the throbbing from his knee.

Everything outside had gone quiet. Very quiet. Then Butcher's voice came clearly through to where they were sprawled.

"Robb, you hear somethin'?"

"What, Sarge?"

"Dunno. Some noise. Sort of a scuffling. From the boat."

Silence while the two cops listened again. Jamie and Cameron held their breath.

"I can't hear anything, Sarge. Perhaps it was the wind?"

"Perhaps." Butcher sounded doubtful. "Just make sure you have a good look around."

Robb's footsteps crunched around the boat and a couple of seconds later Jamie and Cameron heard the scrape of his boots as he dragged himself on board.

It seemed an eternity that the two of them crouched motionless, listening to the cautious creak of footsteps on old timber. Jamie hardly dared to breathe. He wondered what they'd do if Robb came plunging through the deck the same way Cameron had. The constable, however, moved far more cautiously than either of them, testing each board carefully before putting his weight on it.

It must have been fully five minutes before they heard him call to Butcher, his words muffled by two levels of deck.

Butcher's reply though, from just a couple of metres away, was clearly audible.

"Have you looked below?"

A brief answer, obviously in the negative.

"Then bloody well get down there and look around. Why do you think I told you to get your torch?"

Outside, Butcher muttered to himself as Robb's footsteps moved aft towards the hatch. A few seconds later the boards above their heads began to creak. Through the hole Jamie caught the occasional flash of a torch beam probing the dusty darkness. The cop must have been crawling forward in much the same fashion as Jamie had, because no longer could they make out the thud of each footstep. Now he moved with a slow and deliberate scraping motion. Jamie's skin prickled.

The scraping stopped right alongside the hole where Cameron had fallen through, almost directly above their heads. The silence was deafening. Jamie could sense the tension in Cameron's body. He was sure that the other boy was ready to attack if Robb came any further down. Adrenaline pumped through Jamie's system, causing his fingertips to tingle and heightening his awareness of everything around him.

It wasn't necessary for the young cop to climb any further, however. With a sudden, sharp click, a beam of harsh bluish light sliced into the gloom. In the dark hold, the intensity of the light was blinding. Slowly and methodically it probed through the darkness ahead of them, moving inexorably in their direction. Eventually, inevitably, it crossed Cameron's leg, the reflective panels on his running sneaker gleaming white in the beam.

Slowly easing himself a little further into the hole, Robb lifted the beam until it shone directly into Cameron's face. The boy shielded his eyes from the glare. Then the cop swung the beam across onto Jamie. Unlike Cameron, though, Jamie stared straight into the blinding spot, unable to make out anything, but keeping his stare firmly locked on the burning circle of light.

For twenty or thirty seconds, all three froze. Then the light went out. It was like being plunged into the depths of a mine; the darkness was blinding. Bright spots danced across Jamie's vision, and he briefly heard the girl's voice echo somewhere in the back of his head, but he forced it out of his mind.

"Sarge?"

Constable Robb's voice boomed in the stillness.

"Yeah, what?"

The tiniest of pauses.

"There's nothing in here except dust. Can I come out now?"

Butcher grunted his assent and Robb scraped his way back to the hatch. They heard him climb down the side, have a muffled conversation with Butcher somewhere towards the stern, and then a minute or two later the four-wheel drive roared into life and faded away down the beach towards town.

TWELVE

"Careful."

"Damn!"

Jamie's knee throbbed as he eased himself slowly onto the sand alongside the boat.

"How's your knee?" *— ? what did he fall on*

"Sore. I'll get back, though."

"Let me know if you want to take a break."

"Yeah. Let's get movin', eh?"

The two trudged along the beach. They'd stayed in the bottom of the boat, still and silent, for about twenty minutes after four-wheel drive had departed. Eventually Cameron had climbed out, checking that they were alone again. Getting Jamie back down onto the sand with an injured knee had been tricky, but after some lifting and a fair bit of swearing they'd managed it. Neither spoke until they were well clear of the wreck, a few hundred metres back towards town.

"What do you reckon that was all about?"

"No idea. They were looking for something, that's for sure."

"They were lookin' for me."

Cameron nodded. "That's the way I saw it."

"So why didn't Robb turn us in, then?" *i asked myself the same question*

"Don't know. It's difficult to say with Robb. I think it's mainly Butcher who's after you."

"So what's Robb's game?"

"It's hard to guess. He's been here a couple of years now, but nobody knows too much about him. He tends to keep to himself."

"All the time?"

"Pretty much. I heard a rumour that he had some relatives in town, but no one ever sees him down at the pub, or out with people, so it's probably just talk. There was a fair bit of gossip about him when he first arrived."

"How come?"

"He was brought in to replace McPherson. The other cop. You met him yet?"

"Once." Jamie recalled the drunk staggering up the road on his first morning in Port Barren. [he had that confrontation on the way to arch?]

"Yeah, well there's some real problems with him. He used to be a pretty good bloke, but then a few years ago he started goin' on binges. Drinking himself stupid for anything up to a week at a time. Didn't used to do it too often, but in the last year or so he's been getting worse and worse. He still does the odd shift, when he's sober, but a lot of the time he's not much use to anyone. They can't move him, 'cause there's nowhere else will take a drunk copper, and in any case, for some reason Butcher won't let him leave, so they're pretty much just waiting for him to drink himself to death. That's why Robb got posted here — early replacement. He seems to be a pretty straight character by all accounts."

Jamie shrugged. He remembered that night outside the admin building. He was certain that Robb had known that he was there, standing in the darkened street. He considered telling Cameron about the incident, but decided not to. Instead, he changed the subject.

"You reckon there's somethin' special about that boat?" [he is right]

"Special?" Cameron threw him a funny look.

"Yeah. Why would Butcher care that I'd been out there? Jamie suddenly remembered something. "What was that story you were gonna tell me?"

"Story?"

"Back before Butcher arrived — on the boat. You were starting to tell me somethin' — why you wouldn't normally hang around out there."

"Oh yeah, that."

"So?"

Cameron gave a kind of awkward shuffle, avoiding eye contact.

"Like I told you, it's nothing major, only a kid's story."

"About?"

"That boat. There's a bit of history attached to it."

"History?"

"Yeah. Stuff that happened ages ago. Some of the kids round town are a bit superstitious. You know how it is."

"Superstitious?"

"Ghosts. That sort of rubbish." — *not true or silly*

"You sayin' it's haunted?"

"Not haunted exactly, just" — Cameron paused, looking for the right word — "bad. A bad place to hang out."

"How come? What happened?"

Only the crunch of Cameron's shoes on the red sand broke the silence. Jamie limped along next to him, waiting for an answer.

"You know what that boat was?"

"Eh?"

"Does it look familiar to you?"

"The boat?" Jamie tried to imagine where he might have seen it before.

"Not that exact boat obviously, but that type of thing."

Jamie answered with a blank look.

"The shape ..." Cameron tried again. "Does it remind you of anything?"

like in the Prologue

94 ▲

There was something recognisable about the old hulk, Jamie thought. He'd felt that the first night he'd seen it, even in the dark, but he couldn't pin down what it was.

"Perhaps ..."

"Think about the news."

"Eh?"

"On tele."

"When?"

"All the time. You'd see one every couple of months at least."

Jamie finally realised.

"Reffos?"

"Yeah. It was a refugee boat."

"I thought they burned them."

"Not always. Usually they burn them to punish the skip- pers, but in this case it didn't matter."

boat / driver

"How come?"

"The skipper was dead."

Jamie absorbed this.

"What's that got to do with Butcher and Robb?"

Cameron stopped, a serious expression on his face.

"Listen, if I tell you about this you can't mention it to anyone, okay?"

"Why not?"

"Just give us your word that you won't mention it. At all. There's people in town won't appreciate you knowing this story."

"Fine, whatever."

"No, not whatever, I'm dead serious. You won't mention this. Not to Lorraine, not to Archie, not to anyone."

"Okay, I told you, you've got my word."

Cameron stared long and hard at Jamie before speaking. As he began talking they started to move again. Very slowly.

"When I first arrived, there were more kids in Port Barren than nowadays. That's the way things tend to go around here

— sometimes the town is packed, sometimes it's virtually empty. This was four years ago — I was thirteen, and we all used to hang out down at the jetty in the afternoons. You know the one?"

Jamie nodded. *what does that mean*

"Most of the time we'd just be sitting around talking, or kicking a footy or something, pretty harmless stuff. There were a few older kids, probably about the same age as we are now, but they seemed like adults then."

A slight breeze drifted across from the desert, sending ruffles skidding across the surface of the flat sea.

"One afternoon there were about eight or nine of us at the jetty, and this year-eleven guy, Jess, was telling us about a haunted boat he said was parked up the beach. Really talking it up, he was. Reckoned they'd found it all shot up a few years earlier, and that there'd been bodies all over it, and blood soaked into everything. We all thought he was trying to get a reaction out of the younger kids, so we played along with him."

Jamie threw a sideways glance, but Cameron was lost in the memory of that afternoon.

a soccer ball "It was really hot, but we couldn't go in the water because of the stingers, and everyone was pretty bored. No one had the energy to kick the footy, so when someone suggested that we all go and check out this haunted boat, it seemed like a good idea. You know, something to do. A couple of the little kids refused to come. Jess had put the wind up them really badly, but there were still five or six of us prepared to have a look."

A flurry of dust, caught up by the breeze, whipped across the beach, stinging Jamie's bare legs.

"I can't remember how long it took us to walk there. Must have been only fifteen or twenty minutes, same as now, but it seemed a lot longer. All the way, Jess was telling us these stories about the boat."

"How did he know them?"

"He reckoned he'd overheard his dad talking to his mates about it when they were drunk. Said that a few blokes from the town had found it a couple of years earlier, on a fishing trip. Drifting and all shot up, full of bodies. They'd towed it back and then there'd been all sorts of goings on. But I'll get to that." *that could be the guys in the prologue*

"What happened when you got out there?"

"By the time we reached it, everyone was pretty spooked. We'd been working ourselves up, and Jess had done a pretty good job of convincing us that the thing would be soaked in blood and covered in bullet holes. It was a bit of a let-down to find out that it wasn't."

"What happened?"

"A couple of kids started making jokes at Jess for talking it up so much. So he dared one of them to go on board."

"Did they?"

"Yeah, one did." Cameron paused. His brow furrowed in an effort of memory. "A red-headed kid, Andrew his name was. *one of the* He was a total nutter most of the time, real fiery and always *disabled* up for a fight. I heard somewhere that he had problems at home. Must have been fourteen or fifteen then. He fronted *kids?* up to Jess, said he didn't believe a word of it, then turned and walked over to the boat."

There was a long pause.

"We were all pretty nervous. None of us thought he'd actually do it — go on board, I mean. He walked around the back of the boat, and everyone was waiting for him to chicken out. One of the girls was so scared she was crying. But a minute or so later, Andrew appeared up on the deck, grinning like an idiot, and taking the mick out of Jess even more than before."

Cameron stopped. Jamie waited for a few seconds, giving him time to continue, but Cameron remained quiet, too caught up in remembering the story to keep telling it. In the end Jamie prompted him.

"Is that it?"

"Sorry — no. What happened next was what freaked us all out."

"What?"

"We were all relaxing a bit and laughing at Jess when someone grabbed Andrew."

"What?"

"From behind. This figure rose up and grabbed him while he was standing on the deck making fun of Jess."

"Shit! Was he all right?" *disappeared!*

"Oh, yeah. He was fine, but it was late afternoon, and the sun was behind them, so all we could see from the beach was this dark shape grab him and drag him backwards onto the deck. Turned out to be McPherson, but we didn't realise that at the time. All of us just went nuts; a couple of the younger ones burst into tears, one of the girls screamed, and the whole lot of us, including Jess, bolted for town."

"What about Andrew?"

Cameron looked embarrassed.

"We left him there. We were all uptight and nobody even stopped to think. Everyone just ran."

"What happened to him, then?" *One should be first!*

"He turned up at school the next day with a black eye. He was pretty shitty at all of us for taking off. His old man was furious and tried to get McPherson kicked off the force, but Butcher pulled some strings and put a stop to that. In the end the family packed up and left town. I guess he ended up in the city somewhere."

Jamie turned the story over in his head. It was strange, but not strange enough to explain Butcher and Robb's behaviour that afternoon.

"So just because some drunk cop hit a kid there, everyone thinks it's haunted?"

"No. That's just part of it. That's why all the kids stay away from the place. It's become a kind of local myth."

"So what's the rest of it."

Cameron stopped again. As he looked at Jamie, a rare cloud drifted across the sun, briefly taking the glare out of the afternoon, making everything seem curiously undefined.

"This is the bit you can't talk about."

"What?"

"You know the first part? The bit about the fishing trip?" *couldent undstd*

"The young blokes finding the boat drifting?"

"Yeah."

"What about it?"

"Well, it's true. My old man told me about it. After he heard what happened to Andrew, he told me the story as a warning not to go back out there, or to bring it up around school. He said it was a pretty sensitive issue."

"How come?"

" 'Cause the bloke who found the boat and towed it back to town, six years ago, was Port Barren's young new police sergeant, Elliot Butcher." *woah.*

THIRTEEN

"You're kiddin'!"

"No joke. Dad filled me in on what he'd heard around the place, which wasn't a lot but enough to know that a couple of years earlier there'd been some pretty strange events surrounding that boat. We were still new to the town and the last thing he wanted was me making us unpopular by sticking my nose into the town cop's dirty history. That was why he warned me about it."

like what!?

"What's the whole story, then?"

"I don't know all of it."

"Tell me what you do know."

parking lot

Cameron paused, gathering his thoughts again. They'd arrived back at the edge of the townsite, but neither made any attempt to climb up the rocks to the carpark. Instead, they walked in silence to the jetty, the same one that the kids from the town had hung around four years earlier. Once seated in the slatted shade, Cameron continued.

"They reckon it was a refugee boat that was attacked by pirates. You know the type you hear about on the news occasionally? They use machine guns and fast inflatables and attack just about anything that floats, usually in the South

China Sea, or the Straits of Malacca, but sometimes a lot closer to Australia."

"Why would they attack a reffo boat?"

Cameron shrugged. *refugees from wharf*

"They just take whatever they can get. Most of the people on these boats are carrying everything they own with them, so there's probably some family treasures and those sort of things which would be worth a few dollars. Either way, they reckon that's what happened on our boat. Pirates came aboard, machine-gunned everyone, blew up the engines, radios and steering, and took whatever they could find."

"They killed everyone?"

"Almost. The fishing cruiser that found the boat was probably one of those anchored out there." Cameron gestured at the few pleasure craft floating off the beach on their moorings. "There were a few young blokes on board, including the two new town cops — Butcher and McPherson. Our drunk mate. They were the two that went on board and found the bodies."

'Shit! What did they do?"

"As far as Dad knows, they organised a rope and towed the boat back to Port Barren. Butcher was the youngest sergeant in the police force at the time, and he probably thought that bringing the boat back would be good for his career. Turned out to be pretty much the end of it, though."

"Eh?"

"They didn't check the boat properly. There was a survivor — a young girl, nine or ten years old. They found her when they got the boat back here. She didn't speak any English and she was in a pretty bad way. Instead of being impressed, the immigration authorities were furious. They launched a full investigation — that's another reason why they didn't burn the boat; they wanted to have it checked over thoroughly, and they tried to have Butcher charged with neglect for not calling them in immediately. Said they'd have him charged with *what ever happened to the girl!?*

bringing an illegal immigrant into the country if she lived, and that they'd press for manslaughter if she died. Either way, Butcher was in the shit."

"Looks like he managed to get out of it though."

Cameron threw him a look.

"That's where the whole story gets really strange."

"How?"

"The girl needed a lot of attention. She was just about dead, and half out of her mind. No one was sure where she was from, and nobody understood her language. She was put in the nursing station, and the flying doctor was called to bring an interpreter up and to take her back to hospital in the city. An hour or so out of Perth they had engine trouble and had to turn back. It was the following morning by the time they arrived here."

"Then what happened."

"Nothing. The girl was gone."

"Gone?"

"Sometime in the night. She vanished from the nursing station."

"Wasn't someone keeping an eye on her?"

"The town doctor. He said he fell asleep, and when he woke up she'd vanished."

"Didn't they look for her?"

"Apparently. Did a huge search all around the town. Even put the flying doctor back in the air to search, but couldn't find a thing. No one saw her go, no one heard her go. She simply vanished into thin air, and so did Butcher's problems."

"Very convenient."

"Sort of."

"What do you mean?"

"It was the end of his career. Not only was he responsible for bringing her here in the first place, but he was in charge of the search. A few people reckon he never meant to find her, if you know what I mean. No one could prove anything against him, but in the police that sort of thing stays with you, and he's stuck as a sergeant in Port Barren for the rest of his time in the force, that's for sure."

"It still seems pretty strange."

"What does?"

"Why kill your career to get rid of a refugee girl? The worst they could do would be to give Butcher a slap on the wrist. Why would he get rid of her?"

Cameron shook his head. "No idea." *mabey she was evil?*

They sat silently while Jamie turned the story over in his head, trying to put it all together. It didn't add up — Butcher's continuing interest in the old wreck, even now, six years later, or the fact that no one in the town was game to ask about what really went on that day.

"There must be more to it."

Cameron gave him a suspicious glance.

"You said you wouldn't mention this to anyone."

"Yeah, but think about it. Nothing makes sense. Butcher might be a thug but he's not stupid. Why'd he bugger up his whole career for no reason? It doesn't add up. There's got to be more to the story."

The expression on Cameron's face revealed his discomfort.

"I wish I hadn't told you. Forget it, eh? There's nothing more to find out, and if there was, there's no one who'll tell you any more than I already have."

Jamie ignored him, thinking again through the events surrounding the derelict boat. Butcher had something to hide, that was for sure. Obviously, it was to do with the girl that they'd found, something she'd seen, or known, but what? *he could have found some treasure?*

They sat in silence for a long time. Overhead, the sun was starting to drop slowly towards the horizon, and the sky took on the first pink tinges of sunset. It didn't get any cooler though. The wind still blew hot from the desert and whipped up flurries of red sand around them. Images and sounds drifted through Jamie's mind, like distant echoes, fragments of half-remembered events from the past.

the heard a girls voice in his head onetime

Finally Cameron hauled himself slowly to his feet.

"I've gotta go. Mum'll be wondering where I am, and she's gonna kill me anyway for missing my correspondence classes."

He stretched his hand towards Jamie and heaved him upright.

"You know what I reckon?"

"What?"

"I think something else must have happened on that boat. Something Butcher wants to hide."

Cameron shrugged. "Perhaps. But even if there is, I don't see how you'll find out about it."

"Easy."

"How?"

"Ask someone who was there."

"Butcher? You're nuts."

"Not Butcher."

"Then who?"

Jamie looked at Cameron.

"McPherson."

we found treasure

Jamie meets cam on the boat,

FOURTEEN

It was only five-thirty and the pub was quiet.

Jamie stood on the far side of the road looking at the tin and fibro building. He knew the Port Barren pub wouldn't fill until later. Most of the men in town would go home and have dinner before heading out for a couple of beers.

He was alone. Cameron had gone home to face his mother, unimpressed with Jamie's suggestion of speaking to the cop.

"You're mad," had been his response.

Nothing Jamie said could convince Cameron that it would be worth talking to McPherson, and in the end Cameron had headed off, leaving Jamie to wander home to Archie's place.

He hadn't planned to find McPherson, not right away in any case. As he wandered past the pub though, the idea nagged at him until he stopped, leaning on a dusty four-wheel drive and looking thoughtfully at the old shed on the other side of the street.

The Port Barren pub was what used to be called a nissan hut — a long structure with a corrugated iron roof which curved from ground level on one side smoothly across to ground level on the other. It looked a little like a giant water tank, cut in half and laid over on its side. Near the peak of the arched roof an ancient air-conditioner wheezed and splut-

*McPherson could have had an episode thats why hes an alcoholic

tered, fighting a losing battle against the continuous dust and heat.

McPherson would be drinking alone inside. It would be easy for Jamie to stick his head through the door and see. Cameron would kill him and so would Lorraine, and he shuddered to think what would happen if Butcher found him heading into or out of the pub, but even so ...

His mind made up, Jamie glanced in both directions then dashed across the dusty road.

Inside, the pub was little more than a cavernous space with a timber bar at one end. It was dark and surprisingly cool, lit only by a couple of neon lights over the bar and two ineffectual light bulbs hanging high in the roof. Standing just inside the door Jamie waited for his eyes to adapt. The place was almost deserted — only a few shadowy figures, in groups of two or three, sipped at beers and talked quietly. The atmosphere was almost like the inside of a church. At one end of the bar a familiar figure sat alone, hunched over a glass. McPherson, still in his uniform.

Breathing deeply to keep his pulse rate under control, and trying to stay inconspicuous, Jamie picked his way through the gloom.

It was immediately apparent that McPherson wasn't on his first drink for the evening. He wasn't so much sitting on his barstool as using it to prop himself up. Jamie stood a couple of feet behind him, trying to think of a way to approach, when the cop spoke.

"What're you looking at?"

He didn't look around. His speech was slurred with drink. Jamie took a step forward.

"G'day." He tried to keep his voice steady, but in his ears it sounded squeaky and nervous.

"Piss off."

"I'd like to talk to you."

"I said" — the cop turned slowly, and for the first time Jamie could study his face close up — "Piss off!"

He looked old. Years of drink and harsh weather had taken their toll and his skin was weathered and leathery. Two bloodshot eyes glared at him, the neon lights over the bar reflecting in them as a red gleam. Jamie took another tentative half step.

"Can I buy you a drink?"

McPherson swung around to face the bar again, turning his back. He said nothing and after a minute of silence, Jamie's nerves, already stretched to breaking point, were about to crack completely. He was about to leave when McPherson's unsteady voice boomed out again, calling to the barman.

"Jim! Get us another." He waved his almost empty glass in the air. "This bloke's payin'." *he's gonna hear the real story*

The barman gave him a long, hard look as he took the five-dollar note that Jamie proffered. He knew who Jamie was, everyone in town did, but he didn't say anything.

Beer in hand, McPherson settled again onto his barstool. Jamie rested his elbow briefly on the top of the counter, but the wood was sticky with dried beer, and he quickly moved his arm.

"Whadda you want?" McPherson took a long draught from his beer.

"Just a chat."

"'Bout what?"

Jamie took a deep breath.

"The boat up the beach."

McPherson's glass froze in mid-air, halfway to his mouth. He slammed it down, its contents splashing out, and looked around fearfully. Then he half-turned and brought his face in close to Jamie's, his voice little more than a whisper. The smell of stale beer and spirits on his breath made Jamie nauseous.

"You better be careful askin' about that boat. You don't want anyone hearin' you talkin' 'bout that." *? why does noene talk about the boat?*

▲ 107

"Why not?"

The cop looked at him as though he was mad.

"You wanna disappear too? Eh?"

Jamie's heart thumped.

"Why would I disappear?"

Unexpectedly, McPherson laughed.

"You don't know anythin', do you?"

He swung back to the bar, taking another mouthful.

"I know about the girl."

The response was instant and electric. McPherson half choked on his mouthful of beer, spewing a little onto the already soaked bar towel.

"What about her?" The cop was too drunk to disguise the fear and curiosity in his voice. Jamie took a wild guess.

"I know Butcher killed her. I want to know why."

McPherson shook his head. Suddenly he didn't seem quite so drunk.

"Bugger off, eh? Just get lost."

"I'm not leaving until I get some answers."

"Look." McPherson leaned his head in towards Jamie again. This time, Jamie backed away. "The last thing you want is answers. Trust me. You wanna end up dead?"

"Why would I end up dead? What's Butcher got to hide, eh?"

McPherson returned to his drink and tried to ignore Jamie's presence. Jamie persisted.

"Come on, give me a clue at least. You were on the boat with him. What happened out there, eh? What did he do?"

It was futile. McPherson had obviously decided not to say anything more. After standing and staring at the policeman for another full minute Jamie decided to leave. As he turned, the drunk's voice stopped him.

"Hey!"

"What?"

McPherson clambered methodically and awkwardly off his

~ in tve Same tempo

PROPHECS

stool, every movement painstakingly slow. He staggered across and grabbed Jamie's arm. His voice was a scared whisper with a clarity behind his words that belied his drunken state.

"Listen to me carefully, kid. That girl wasn't the first person Butcher killed that day, and if you keep asking questions there'll be another body somewhere out in the desert for us to look for. Now do us all a favour, piss off and mind your own business, okay?" ✳ Killed more than one person!

"But ..." Before Jamie could press him any further, McPherson shoved him roughly away and returned to his stool and his beer. Toying briefly with the idea of pushing for more information, Jamie thought the better of it.

"I'll come back later. With Cameron."

While Jamie was making his way slowly from the dark, cave-like pub, the barman, who had watched the whole exchange with interest, picked up the phone, dialled, and spoke briefly. ✳ M.

A few minutes later, when Jamie was almost back at Archie's place, the police truck pulled up in front of the pub and Butcher went inside. He emerged soon after, half dragging, half supporting the reeling figure of Constable Mike McPherson.

✳ McPherson DID have a horrifying episode, thats why hes a drunn

Jamie goes to see McPherson. Buys him a beer to talk. McPherson gets draged out of the bar by Sarge B.

FIFTEEN

The ten-minute walk from the pub to Archie's place seemed to pass in an instant as Jamie tried to make some sort of sense of everything. About the boat, the girl, and McPherson's comments. In his mind he could picture the events that Cameron had laid out for him. It was difficult to think of Butcher as anything other than enormous, but with a little imagination he could picture him leaping across to the deserted boat and poking around. He could imagine the scene — bodies piled up and decomposing, Butcher ordering McPherson around, the boat being towed up to the Port Barren jetty, and the girl being discovered and brought ashore, nothing more than a bundle of rag-clad skin and bones, barely alive.

This was where his imagination abandoned him. He couldn't picture her wandering off into the desert in the middle of the night. He could see her unconscious in the nursing station, with the doctor dozing outside the door, but that was it. When he tried to turn his mind to her waking up, unsure and uncertain, and creeping out into the vast, waiting desert, the image refused to come. What came instead was the trapped and helpless feeling he'd experienced while he'd been locked in the oven-hot cage on the police truck.

What had happened on that boat? McPherson's words echoed in his memory — she "wasn't the first person Butcher killed that day". So there was another. On the boat. It was the only explanation. Butcher had to get rid of the girl, and quickly — the flying doctor was bringing an interpreter up with him. That was what Butcher was scared of.

"Shit!" Jamie stopped and sucked in a huge breath of dusty air. In the west, the last gleam of sunset was dying, casting a bloody scar across the sky. A dark stillness was settling — the thick, suffocating heaviness of a Port Barren night. Motionless in the middle of the road, Jamie suddenly knew why he felt so uneasy. It was the girl. It was her voice which seemed to speak into the centre of his brain at times.

The voice! The first time he'd heard it was as he halluci- nated on the brink of unconsciousness in the police cage. Then he'd heard it later that same night — in his bed in the nursing station. The third time was just a few hours ago, when trapped below the decks of the boat. Was the girl speaking to him? It was insane. More than that, it was impossible. He tried to put the idea from his mind, but something told him that he was right — it was her he was hearing.

"Don't be a dickhead," he muttered. "What would Eddie say if you told him that a dead reffo girl was talking to you?" It didn't require a lot of thought.

He'd piss himself laughing and then never let me hear the end of it, Jamie thought. That's what he'd do. Even so, as he started walking again, Jamie hadn't managed to convince himself. Not properly. Still thinking, he turned up the path- way to Archie's house.

The front door was open. That wasn't unusual. Unlike the other inhabitants of Port Barren, Archie seemed to live his life unconcerned about the threat of intrusion. Initially, Jamie had found it disconcerting. At all his other foster homes there'd been locks on the doors and windows. In a couple of the houses it had actually been impossible to get outside without a key. Jamie hadn't managed to stay in either place long enough to be entrusted with one. After a week in Port Barren, however, he'd come to terms with the fact that at Archie's he could come and go as he pleased. And so could anyone else.

Not that anyone ever did. Visitors, invited or uninvited, were rare. So when he heard the voices inside, Jamie stopped on the porch. He couldn't make out the words but someone was talking with Archie, or at least talking to Archie.

He let the flyscreen bang shut behind him as he entered, a warning to whoever was there. It worked — the conversation stopped. There was a moment of silence and the sound of the door echoed in his ears. Jamie stood and waited, alone in the dark passageway.

Footsteps, two or three. Quick, short and anxious. Lorraine appeared in the kitchen doorway. In the rectangle of light cast into the passage, her shadow fell in a long silhouette across the bare floorboards.

"Thank God! Where have you been all afternoon?"

Her voice trembled with barely concealed anger. Jamie shrugged. He didn't need this now.

"Get in here!"

She stepped aside to let him pass into the kitchen. Archie was sitting at the old laminex table, an empty teacup clasped in his hand. Another chair stood opposite him, slightly askew, with an untouched cup in front of it. The brown liquid looked cold and uninviting. Jamie could see the scummy layer of skin that had formed on top.

"Sit down." Jamie would have preferred to stand, but it was a command, not a request. Something in her voice made him obey. Lorraine remained on her feet. She paced for a couple of seconds, her footsteps ringing hollow on the bare floor, before she rounded on him.

"Have you any idea how many people have been looking for you this afternoon?"

Jamie shrugged. All he felt was an overwhelming weariness.

"I've been worried sick. So has Mr Scott. So has Archie."

Jamie's silence infuriated the social worker.

"Say something, for God's sake. At least tell me where you've been. Please." *Is he gonna tell her about the girl?*

Her movements were agitated and seemed strangely out of character. Jamie watched her pace up and down — flicking strands of hair from her face as she moved. Her anger was genuine — no doubt about that. He wondered, though, whether she was concerned about him, or about what he might have discovered. In any case he had to say something.

"Sorry."

"Sorry? Do you know what you've put me and Archie through this afternoon? I should hope you're sorry. That's the least I'd expect. But it's not enough. Where've you been?"

"At the beach."

"Doing what?"

"Messing around. With Cameron."

Lorraine stopped, mid pace. Her expression seemed to change slightly; perhaps it softened a little.

"I went to the school this afternoon. Mr Scott told me you'd gone home sick."

"I did."

"Then why didn't you come home?"

Explaining seemed too difficult. Jamie shrugged.

"Jamie?" Lorraine looked at him. *✱ What time is it?*

"I started to. I just got ..." He struggled to find the word "distracted". He didn't want to lie to her. That could end up creating more problems in the long run, but he wasn't ready to tell her the truth either.

In any case, his half-answer had some effect. She sat heavily on the other chair, her hand closing instinctively around the mug of cold, scummy tea. She made no move to drink it.

"Jamie, you know how much is riding on your behavior here. Do I have to remind you?"

Jamie shook his head.

"Then you must realise how stupid what you did this afternoon was. What if the police find out you were wagging school?" ~~wagging~~ *~itching~*

Jamie almost smiled. If only she knew. He managed to control himself, though, and let her continue.

"Another half an hour and I was going to call Sergeant Butcher in to look for you. We both know what that would have meant."

"Sorry."

Lorraine let go of the cup and reached across, taking his hand on the table. Her touch was light with a faint trace of warmth, perhaps the last heat from the tea, perhaps not. Either way, Jamie felt his skin tingle — it reminded him of his mother. A long time ago. Jamie forced the memories out of his mind. He needed to stay focused.

"Jamie. Please ..." Lorraine stopped.

For a long time the three of them sat, Jamie keeping his face impassive as he struggled with the emotions that stormed around inside him, Lorraine looking at him, appraising, Archie sitting silently, watching.

"Are you all right?" Lorraine asked finally. *X Jamie is in a tough position*

"Yeah, I'm fine." The wave subsided and Jamie began to feel in control again. Archie filled the kettle and replaced it on the old stove. Releasing Jamie's hand, Lorraine leaned back from the table.

"What were you doing down there? You're filthy."

"Nothin' much. Talkin' mainly."

"Talking?"

"Yeah."

There was a moment of silence. Jamie waited.

"What did you talk about?"

"Bits and pieces." A thought came to him — Lorraine must

have been around Port Barren for a few years now. "Cops and boats, mainly."

Her whole attitude changed. Her body stiffened as she sat up suddenly, throwing him a penetrating stare. For a moment Jamie thought that she was going to press him for more details and he dropped his eyes, ready to go quiet if needed. Lorraine hesitated then decided not to press the issue, at least for the moment.

he did fall and hurt himself

"You'd better go and wash up."

Jamie nodded and rose silently. As he moved towards the door, Lorraine noticed the deep scratches on his arm, a legacy of his awkward fall into the bottom of the boat. She saw the dried blood in the cuts. She noticed the limp.

"What happened to you? Have you been fighting?"

"Nah." Jamie shook his head, struggling to find a plausible explanation. "I just had a bit of a fall. From the rocks near the car park."

Lorraine looked him up and down again. He could tell she didn't believe him.

"Go and get cleaned up, and then let me have a look at those cuts."

As he reached the kitchen door, he turned back to face Lorraine and Archie, who were still sitting at the kitchen table. Lorraine was watching him with a slightly worried frown. The little crease between her eyes, which always appeared when something was on her mind, was obvious in the bright glare of the kitchen bulb.

"Can I ask a question?"

Archie raised an eyebrow. Lorraine answered right away.

"Sure. Of course."

"Was McPherson a drunk when he arrived in Port Barren?" Lorraine looked confused.

"What? Jamie, I hardly think …"

"Go wash." Archie spoke the words quietly, with just the tiniest of nods towards the door. There was no room for

Archie finally spoke!

hesitation — it was clearly a command. Jamie grinned to himself as he left the room.

SIXTEEN

"Hey!"

Jamie sat up in bed, startled to find Cameron at the back door.

"What's happening?" *gonna talk about the boat

"Nothin'. Come in."

Cameron climbed the stairs and walked inside, taking in the screened-in porch with a quick glance.

"Nice place."

"It's comfy."

"Yeah."

While Cameron pulled an old wooden chair up towards the bed, Jamie propped himself on one arm.

"Haven't seen you for a day or two."

"I've been keepin' out of the way. After the boat and that." He didn't mention his conversation with McPherson. Now wasn't the time. *he should tell him about the conversation

"Yeah. How'd you hold up the other night?"

"Not too bad."

"I slept like a log." Cameron grinned. "Must have been that lucky punch you got in."

"Lucky?"

"Yeah. You wait — next time I'll be ready for you."

"You're just soft." Jamie began to feel a little less morose. He'd been feeling strange since waking up, an hour or so ago. It was Saturday morning so school wasn't an issue, but Jamie was bored, and even school would have at least been something to do. In the few days since the episode at the boat he'd been continuing his policy of lying low, so there wasn't *What is that?* anywhere he could go. He was pleased to see Cameron's face grinning up through the fly wire. The two of them hadn't spoken much since that afternoon. At school Cameron always seemed to be hanging around with the other kids, and Jamie didn't feel like dealing with all the stares and whispers, so apart from a couple of nods the two of them had stayed away from one another.

"You heard the news?" Cameron was serious again.

"What news?"

"About McPherson."

"Eh?" Jamie sat up. "What about him?"

"He's dead. Topped himself."

"Bullshit!"

"Nah. Hung himself from the lamp pole on the end of the jetty. They found him last night."

"When did he do it?" *BUTCHER DID IT!*
Cameron shrugged.

"Dunno. No one had seen him for a couple of days. Last time anyone saw him was the other night in the pub."

"Which night?" Jamie's heart began to pound.

"Wednesday, same day as the boat thing."

Jamie felt the blood draining from his face.

"Shit mate. I'm in trouble."

"Eh? What?"

"I was talkin' to him, McPherson." *no it was*

"When?"

"The other day. After you headed home." *butcher*

Jamie related his trip to the pub. When he'd finished speaking, Cameron sat for a couple of minutes.

"Bloody hell, mate. What do you think he meant?"

"I reckon there must have been someone else on the boat. Butcher knocked them off and didn't know about the girl bein' there. Maybe she saw somethin'. He was just lucky she didn't speak English, but he had to get rid of her too, before the flying doctor arrived with an interpreter." *thats exactly*

Cameron thought about this, then nodded. *What happened*

"Yeah. Makes sense. What about McPherson though?"

Jamie shook his head.

"That's what worries me. He tells me this the other night, or at least gives me a few pretty simple clues, and then suddenly he's dead. You really reckon he killed himself?"

"Don't know. Couple of guys found him when they went fishing. No idea how long he'd been there, but the doctor said it couldn't have been more than a couple of hours."

"So where'd he go then? Between Wednesday and last night?"

"God knows." *butcher took him out of the Pub*

Jamie's head was whirling with ideas and suspicions. The uneasy sensation was stronger and more intense than ever. It reminded him of something else he'd meant to discuss.

"I been thinkin' —"

"Yeah? Did it hurt?"

"Nah serious. 'Bout somethin' you said."

"What?"

"The other day, out on the boat, when we were talkin', you said that everyone felt strange when they arrived here. Remember?"

Cameron's expression changed.

"Yeah. I was hoping you'd forgotten about that."

"You got any idea why?"

"Why?"

"Why everyone feels that way?"

"Listen ..." Cameron stopped, gathering his thoughts.

"You'll think this is a bit weird. Anyway, it's just a theory of mine. Nothing I could prove."

"What?"

"You ever been to that old prison down in the city?"

"Don't change the subject."

"I'm not. You ever been there?"

"Which one?" There were several prisons and Jamie had visited his brother in a few of them.

"The museum one, down near the port."

"You mean that old one, built by convicts?"

"Yeah."

"Nah, never been there." That had been closed down long before Eddie got put away.

"We went to visit it during our holidays. They take you on tours."

"So?"

"So there's this one cell you visit — right near the gallows. When I went into it I felt totally freaked out. A bit like when you go near the boat only more intense." ~what did he do?!

"Yeah. So what's your point?"

"The tour guide was telling us about how they used those little cells for the death inmates, the ones due for hanging. There was a whole tiny row of them there, but only this one cell got to me. It turned out to be the one where the condemned prisoners were locked on their own for the last three hours before they were executed." ※ mabey he has a 6th sence

Jamie considered this.

"So what? I don't get it."

"My point is this, and this is my theory so you better not laugh, even though it sounds stupid. I reckon that places absorb some sort of energy from the people who live in them. You know how in some places you automatically feel welcome and happy, and in others you don't? Well, that's what I think causes it. And anywhere that people have been through a lot of pain there's a really potent build-up of that energy."

"You're talkin' about ghosts." [handwritten: or move like spirits]

"No, it's not really ..." Cameron thought for a second. "Well yeah — I guess you could say that, but not like walking sheets and rattling chains and that stuff. This is more, I don't know, more abstract. This isn't something that can harm you or anything. It's just an energy field that you can sense. That's all."

"What's this got to do with Port Barren?"

"It's got more to do with that boat."

"Eh?"

"Think about it. That little girl they found on board. How long had she been lying there with her family and friends shot up all around her? Imagine how scared she'd have been. Couldn't the boat have picked up on that?"

"So you do reckon it's haunted." [handwritten: * Definitely haunted]

"I knew you'd think it was funny." Cameron stood up, unhappy.

"Nah. It's just" — Jamie looked for the right word — "weird. Makes sense though in a strange kind of way." Jamie thought about the other places he'd felt the girl's presence — the back of the truck, the nursing station.

"Anyway," Cameron continued, "it's just this idea I had. It's not like you could prove it or anything."

"Nah. Guess not."

Cameron obviously wanted to change the subject.

"You want to do something?"

"What?"

"Don't know. Go down the beach and hang out. Always a few guys under the jetty of a Saturday morning."

The feeling of being an outcast in the town was still strong in Jamie's mind, and since the incident with the windows it had been more uncomfortable than ever being around people. He'd heard the whispers and the sniggers behind his back, and in school the odd comment, pitched just loud enough for him to hear. It was too much effort to deal with other kids.

▲ 121

Besides all of that, he had a feeling that if Butcher had discovered what he and Cameron had worked out, then both of them were in danger, but Jamie in particular — he was the only one who'd actually been seen talking to McPherson that night. If word got back to Butcher ...

"Nah, she'll be right. You go."

"You'll have to start mixing with the others at some point, you know." *(Why have homework?)*

"It's not just that, I got homework to do. Gotta catch up."

For a second or two Cameron looked like he was going to argue, and then decided against it.

"Whatever. I'm going to head off. If you change your mind ..."

He left the sentence unfinished. They both knew there was no chance of that happening.

"I might catch you a bit later, eh?"

"Yeah, sure."

"See ya."

The screen door slammed and Cameron was gone. *maybe*

Cameron went to Jamies house. He told him that McPherson is dead Jamie tells cameron that the boat is haunted

SEVENTEEN

Jamie moped around the house, bored and restless. Cameron was right. He couldn't just hang around on his own forever, but he found it hard to go anywhere in Port Barren. It wasn't just the kids. Everywhere he went he was aware of the accusing glances, the pointed stares. Even though there wasn't a shred of evidence against him, he knew that in the minds of the people of Port Barren he was guilty of the window vandalism, and who knew what else. Also, of course, the possibility of running into Butcher worried him. In fact, when he thought about it, he was a little disturbed that Butcher had been so quiet for the last couple of days. If the Sergeant was actually aware of what Jamie had discovered, then it was surprising that Jamie hadn't already had a visit. The thought played on his mind.

why do the hate him so much

He started a bit of reading, part of his homework, but the conversation with Cameron kept turning over and over in his mind. In the end he flopped off his bed and wandered into the kitchen, where Archie was sitting in his usual seat at the table, reading the paper.

What does archie do all day!?

"Morning."

Archie nodded without looking up.

"You got anythin' needs doin' round the place?"

He wasn't sure why he'd asked. It seemed better than hanging around doing nothing. Archie put down the paper and turned his level gaze upwards. Once again Jamie found himself uncomfortably aware of those blue eyes, so out of place on Archie, and the feeling that they were staring deep into his soul. *sounds like a scary guy*

"Sit down." Again the low, resonant voice seemed to go right through Jamie. He pulled up a chair.

"You want to hear a story?" *finally we get to hear archie?*

"Eh?"

"This town, it's full of stories. Some Aboriginal, some white, some Malay, some Indonesian. All sorts of different ideas. I reckon you might need to hear one of them."

Jamie shrugged his shoulders. This wasn't what he'd expected.

"I've got nothin' better to do."

"No, not good enough." Archie stared again. "I talk only to people who want to listen."

Under the searching gaze Jamie felt increasingly uncomfortable. Without realising it he fidgeted slightly.

"Sorry."

"Why?"

"I just am."

Archie continued to stare, until Jamie couldn't handle it any longer.

"Tell me the story. Please. I want to hear it."

The old man held his gaze steady for a few seconds longer, then turned his attention back to the newspaper. Guessing that he'd said the wrong thing, Jamie started to leave. Archie's voice shattered the silence like a gunshot.

"Sit!"

The single word seemed to echo off all the hard surfaces in the room and Jamie sunk back into the chair. Without taking his eyes off the paper, Archie began to speak.

"You come into this town thinking that you're something

different, something new. But you're not, you know. People have been coming and going from this part of the country for much longer than either you or I have been around. All for different reasons. First the Aborigines. They came for their dreaming, to visit their sacred places, to hunt, for ceremonies. Then when time had passed and the seasons began to change they'd leave for a while — move on to other parts. Later the white men arrived — came for old rocks buried in ancient ground. Came to dig and to load onto ships. When the rocks are gone, so are they."

maybe thats where all the feelings come from?

Archie sipped his tea.

"Oh yes, son. This land's had its share of weary travellers. The locals have names for them. Two main types, we say — wanderers, and lost ones." *like Jamie?*

Jamie sat still, interested but not wanting to show it.

"Many lost ones and many wanderers have come, and many have left again. Some at peace, some in turmoil. Some are people who were taken from where they belonged. These are the wanderers — people searching for their homes. Some are those who had the place they belong to taken from them. These are the lost ones. They search for a new place to belong. Sooner or later though, they all seem to come to Port Barren."

Archie's voice was deep, almost rhythmic. Jamie felt himself being drawn into the story.

"Not so many years ago, the wanderers started to come from the south. These were Aborigines — the Punjima, the Kurrama and the Innawonga peoples. The stolen children, and their children. They began to return to the place of their birth, of their dreaming. They returned to walk the land of their ancestors, to join with the spirits of the earth that bore them.

The lost ones came more recently, from the sea, from far-off places and distant wars. They landed all up and down the coast. Many had been promised paradise — a land of oases and palm trees, of cool, deep, green waters. What they found was desert and prisons.

To live here, you have to learn that life is a balance between being a wanderer and being a lost one. When these others arrive, in buses and cars or sometimes even on foot from the south, or on old boats from the north, the people who live here can usually make them welcome, because up here everyone is aware of the wanderer and the lost one within themselves. Usually these travellers, wherever they're from, can find peace of some sort. This is important. It keeps the balance of the land.

Archie was a lot to say,

Sometimes, though, there is no peace. A wanderer arrives and is driven away. A lost one comes and yet still remains lost. Then the balance is interrupted. Their pain settles across the land. When this happens, the people must wait for another to come — a wanderer or a lost one who can balance the pain. Can restore the land. Can bring peace."

Jamie struggled to make sense of what the old man was talking about. He knew that there was something in it. It had to do with the girl in the boat, and perhaps even Cameron's strange theory. The two stories sounded sort of similar. Archie had stopped speaking. *he probably does a lot of thinking.*

"Is that it?"

"That's just the start." Archie went quiet again, until finally Jamie had to break the silence.

"So how's it finish then?"

Again the stare.

"That," said Archie, "is up to you."

The old man took a sip of his tea and started to read his paper again. Jamie sat thinking for a few moments longer, then got up and left the kitchen. Flopping onto his bed he tried to decipher the story. It was weird — no beginning, no middle, no end, no plot. And yet he couldn't shake the feeling that there was something important behind the strange words. He pondered it but couldn't make anything of it.

"Bunch of crap," he finally announced, though not loud enough to be heard from the kitchen.

The day passed and the temperature climbed. The rest of the house was insulated, but over Jamie's bed there was only the corrugated tin roof between him and the sun. Eventually, bored and unable to take the heat any longer, Jamie pulled on a tee-shirt and went outside. In the backyard he stood under the rusted Hills hoist and looked at the desert stretching out in front of him. Two thousand kilometres of nothing.

Where the backyard ended was a thick barrier of scrub. Dry, thorny bushes formed a natural, almost impenetrable wall of spinifex. In Archie's yard there'd at least been a token effort to keep the scrub further back than the washing line and the old water tank. Jamie wandered along the edge of the yard until he spotted a small game track between the bushes. The spiny brush scratched and caught at his legs and thighs as he pushed his way through. He flinched as a thorny twig buried itself in the soft flesh of his lower leg. Thinking it might have been a snake bite, he stopped to examine the wound. It was bleeding slightly, but on closer inspection it proved to be little more than a scratch. Jamie pressed on again through the scrub, and after five or six metres he found himself standing at the edge of a large patch of red sand.

He was in the desert.

A couple of steps and he sank into the red dirt up to his ankles. It was roasting hot and filled his sneakers, burning his feet and calves.

"Shit!" Hopping around, he tried to shake the sand out and only partially succeeded. Slowly, though, his feet grew accustomed to the increased temperature and he meandered through the scrub, sticking to the edges of the sandy patches and moving steadily south, away from the town.

Under the constant glare of the sun the landscape took on a strange quality, as though he was standing in the middle of a huge painting. Everything seemed flat and two-dimen-

▲ 127

sional. The horizon appeared to be at once a thousand kilometres away and right in front of him. Pushing through the thick patches of scrub and spinifex, the thought of snakes crossed his mind, but the threat remained somehow unreal, like the landscape itself. *is he dreaming? ? ?

Jamie wandered for about an hour. It might have been more — he had forgotten his watch, and the desert glare seemed to affect his sense of time. A tree of some kind crouched against the enormous horizon off to his left, and he gradually worked his way across towards it. It was scarcely more than a few ragged, stick-like branches clinging to an emaciated trunk, barely thicker than the limbs themselves. Here and there a dusty, murky green leaf fluttered uneasily in the light stirrings of hot air. It wasn't much of a tree, but it was life, thought Jamie, amazed that anything could survive in the thin, dry, baked dirt.

Easing himself to the ground, Jamie rested gently against the trunk. It flexed slightly under his weight.

He tried to picture the girl wandering lost in this inhospitable, sandy wilderness. It was impossible to believe that she'd even managed to get away from the town, through that first barrier of scrub that lined the roadsides and yards.

They'd been promised paradise — a land of oases and palm trees, of cool, deep, green waters. The words from Archie's story came floating unbidden into his mind.

"Yeah, right." Not a lot of that out here.

Stretching out, he closed his eyes and tried to imagine himself a thousand kilometres from Port Barren, not on the edge of the Great Sandy Desert but out in the middle. Away from Butcher, the other kids, and the constant tightness in his guts. Lying there he became aware of the sounds of the desert. The gentle rustle of the bushes as the beginnings of the afternoon wind stirred at their branches. The occasional click of an insect. A louder noise made him sit up. what?

On the other side of the clearing, startled into stillness by

Jamie's sudden movement, stood a racehorse goanna, staring at him. For seconds that seemed to stretch into hours, Jamie and the goanna remained motionless, each eyeing the other warily, until the reptile whirled and vanished in a blur of movement. The only signs it left of its presence were a trembling branch and tiny footprints in the hot, red sand.

The sounds of the desert washed over Jamie. The tightness inside his chest seemed to have gone, perhaps because he was a fair way out, on the other side of town from the boat. Cameron's story about the prison in the city drifted into his mind. That's really what Port Barren was meant to be for him. A prison. A place for the court to send him to keep him out of the way and out of trouble. But he thought about Eddie, locked in a steel and concrete cell, with barred windows and doors and suddenly even Port Barren didn't seem so bad. For the first time since arriving in the town, Jamie felt at ease. Gradually, without even realising it, he drifted off to sleep.

EIGHTEEN

lossed (handwritten, crossed out)

It was the noise that woke him. Not the occasional rustles and clicks that he'd heard in the still heat of the day, but the chirping of cicadas. Thousands and thousands of them. He opened his eyes and a myriad of stars glowed in the sky above him. It was dark.

"Oh shit!" *One might get lossed* (handwritten)

Beneath him the sand was still warm. The moon was rising over the southern horizon, full and blood red, and in the sky the stars gleamed with an intensity that Jamie had never experienced before. Somewhere off in the distance a dingo howled, perhaps inspired by the rising moon. The mournful sound carried through the still air as Jamie leapt to his feet.

His first reaction was one of panic — that he'd not be able to find his way home in the dark. However, a bloom of light filled the horizon in front of him. The lights of Port Barren. Against the desert night, the few streetlights and house lights cast a reassuring glow.

Jamie started directly towards the town, but soon found his way blocked by a large clump of spinifex. It took a couple of minutes to find a way around it, and then seconds later he was confronted with another patch. In the dark it was impossible to spot the tiny game trails that he'd used that afternoon and he was forced to walk long detours.

He'd begin to follow a path through the scrub and then it would run into an enormous clump of spinifex and end abruptly. This meant that he would have to backtrack and make his way to where the ground was more open, continuing in this way around the edge of the scrub. Again and again he came to dead ends — it was like being in a darkened labyrinth of thorny walls. *i knew he was lost*

However, the glow was coming slowly closer. He guessed that his route was taking him around the edge of town, but as long as he kept moving towards the lights he knew he'd be safe.

Even so it was a long time before he pushed through the last patch of scrub and found himself by the highway on the opposite side of the town from Archie's place. A ten-minute walk through the streets of Port Barren and he'd be safely home in bed.

He glanced instinctively towards his left wrist, forgetting that his watch was beside his bed at Archie's place. It must have been pretty late. The roads were still and silent, as were the houses. Even the pub was closed.

He hoped that Archie hadn't worried about him or waited up. The old man noticed everything he did, every time he came and went, but he never commented. It was strange being able to make decisions for himself. It took some getting used to. In the past, everything had been decided for him — by his mum, by his foster parents, by Eddie and finally by the court. For him to be able to make up his own mind was a new experience. What Jamie couldn't work out was whether or not Archie worried about him. Creeping through the night, that was his biggest concern. *he might run into botao*

As he made his way past the school, however, that concern was driven abruptly from his thoughts. A movement down near the end classroom caught his attention. Ducking into the

▲ 131

shadow of a parked Landrover, he watched from across the road as someone crouching low to the ground hurried around the side of the building and stopped for a minute in the deep shadows under the verandah. The figure stood and Jamie drew in a sharp breath. Only one person in Port Barren was that size. Butcher took a few steps out into the square of the playground, in the moonlight there was no doubting his identity.

"What's that bastard up to?"

No sooner had the whispered words passed Jamie's lips than there was a spark, and a tail of fire streaked across the ground from where Butcher stood. For the briefest of seconds the night seemed to stand still, and then a loud "WHUMP!" shattered the silence, as the side of the school erupted into a wall of flame. ✓ he might leave it on Jamie

Breathless, uncertain, staying deep in the shadows, Jamie watched the chaos develop across the road. The flames took only seconds to find their way into the timber supports for the verandah and the wooden beams that held up the floor and roof. The entire building was being consumed. As the dry wood began to combust faster, the roof started to sag and the whole structure began to creak. Against the evil red and yellow light, some of the internal supports stood out clearly, the heat twisting the prefabricated steel into tortured, skeletal shapes. ← What is that?

Even from across the road Jamie could feel the heat on his face. He watched in horrified awe as a column of flame shot high into the still night. Air was sucked into the inferno with a rushing, roaring sound, and there was the occasional explosion of glass as windows burst into fragments, the shards glinting in the light as they were flung outwards into the playground.

Butcher was nothing more than a black silhouette against the inferno, standing with his arms crossed. It was easy to imagine the tiny smile twitching at the corners of his mouth.

The fire continued to grow, and Jamie became so caught up

in watching it that when he next looked for Butcher he was nowhere to be seen. Jamie noticed the lights came on in the house behind him.

"Shit!"

He had to run. His only concern now was to be nowhere nearby when people arrived. Somewhere up the street a car door slammed, an engine fired up and roared off into the darkness. Jamie crept further back into the shadows away from the fire as people started to come out of their houses, dressed in tattered gowns and shorts, pulling on tee-shirts and rubbing sleep from their eyes. *what did he light?*

A couple of streets away he began to move more quickly, confident that anybody who was awake would be moving towards the school, not going in his direction. Stopping on one occasion, he glanced back to where, over the top of the houses, the column of flame and smoke was clearly visible as it leaped into the darkness.

Five or six minutes of jogging in the shadows saw Jamie turning the final corner at the end of Archie's street. He relaxed. The house stood clear in the moonlight a couple of hundred metres away, a dull glow reflecting off the rusted tin roof. The windows were dark and he assumed that Archie was fast asleep in bed; he'd have no trouble creeping in through the back door. Casting a last glance over his shoulder, Jamie saw that the flames from the school were already dying, the inferno consuming itself almost as fast as it had grown.

With home in sight, some of the tension drained from Jamie's shoulders and neck. A last quick survey of the neighborhood revealed everything still and silent, as it should be. Jamie suddenly felt very tired. *why did butcher do that?*

He jogged down the side of the road, moving faster now but still keeping his footsteps as silent as possible.

About five metres from the front gate a spotlight beam sliced through the night and trapped him in its merciless glare.

▲ 133

flaherety's Curse

NINETEEN

"Well, look who we have here."

Butcher's tone was light and cheerful.

[handwritten: was trying to frame him]

"I'd say you're in a little bit of trouble, son."

Transfixed, Jamie blinked and stayed silent his mind almost as paralysed as his body. After the initial shock of discovery he tried to think of a plan, an approach, a way to deal with the situation. Nothing came. The only thought that ran through his mind was how close he'd come to the front gate. Another few steps and he'd have been home. He realised with a shock that even though he'd done nothing wrong he felt strangely guilty. Innocent or not, Jamie knew he was in trouble.

Butcher moved out from behind the police truck that was parked behind a thicket of scrub opposite Archie's house. The spotlight stayed locked unwaveringly on Jamie. He sensed rather than saw the movement of the cop and for a brief second toyed with the thought of escape. [handwritten: what does that mean?]

"Don't bother trying to do a runner," said Butcher, as though reading Jamie's thoughts. "I wouldn't want to have to shoot you, would I?" The tone of his voice made it clear that there was nothing he'd like better. Jamie remained still and silent. The adrenaline coursing through his system heightened his senses, he picked up the crunch of footsteps on gravel as the large cop approached.

"Imagine that. The school catches fire, and not ten minutes later I find you creeping home like a dog with your tail between your legs. Pretty convenient, eh?" *blame it on him*

Butcher loomed out of the glare, directly in front of him. His bulk blocked out the direct beam, throwing Jamie into a darkness almost as blinding as the light. With the beam of the spotlight behind him, Butcher appeared as nothing more than a dark silhouette, framed by an intense corona. His expression was hidden by shadow, but Jamie knew that the now familiar, cold, emotionless little smile would be curling at the corners of Butcher's mouth. The policeman was holding his nightstick in his right hand and slapping it into his left.

we saw Butcher light the fire

"You got anything to say for yourself, son?"

Butcher's voice was low, confident, amused. It reminded Jamie of all the cops and judges and social workers that he'd ever had dealings with. His smug arrogance made Jamie angry and scared at the same time. He stared right at Butcher.

"I didn't burn the school."

He stepped sideways out of the beam, into the protection of the darkness.

The sudden movement caught Butcher unawares. Thinking that Jamie was making a break for it, he lashed out with the steel truncheon, but the club whistled harmlessly through the air. For an instant, Jamie could make out the expression on Butcher's face. It was not only one of anger but also confusion and something resembling fear. He mirrored Jamie's movement, also stepping out of the light so that the two of them stood face to face in the semi-darkness.

"Bullshit," said the cop. "Who did then?"

"You. I saw everything."

The grin faded, but only briefly.

"That'll do you a lot of good in court. Your word against

mine. You really think a judge is gonna believe a teenage piece of dirt like you over a sergeant in the police force?" *[handwritten: need to find evenen]*

"He might."

"You're dreaming." Butcher attempted to sound amused, but Jamie thought he detected a note of fear behind the policeman's words.

"Depends on what I could tell him."

"You? Don't make me laugh. You wouldn't know your arse from a hole in the ground, son. What could you say to make a judge believe you over me?"

"I could tell him about a girl on a boat."

The words were out before Jamie thought about what he was saying. Deathly, total silence followed the comment. The night seemed to hold its breath while Butcher almost imperceptibly tightened his grip on the nightstick.

"What was that?"

Jamie knew he'd trapped himself. He kept speaking, trying to buy a chance to escape, to gain himself a little space.

"I could tell him about the chat I had with McPherson in the pub the other night."

It was a shot in the dark. Butcher's face grew huge as he leaned over to peer closely at Jamie.

"You dumb little bastard." *[handwritten: ✱ he might try to kill Jamie]*

The nightstick lashed out and there was an explosion of light behind Jamie's eyes. He didn't even feel himself hit the ground.

White pain swept through his body, spasms jerked his muscles and his head pounded. Consciousness returned slowly. He was tied up — hands bound behind his back, his feet lashed firmly together at the ankles. It was dark. Not pitch black, but a strange, bluish, flickering darkness. Spots and streaks of imagined light danced across Jamie's vision. From somewhere distant, voices crept into the edges of his awareness — someone yelling, someone else talking normally. He tried to call out. Nothing. His mouth worked against the wad of material that had been forced into it, but it was firmly held in place with a strong cloth that was tied around the back of his head. His stomach churned and Jamie felt the bile rising in his throat. If he vomited, he'd drown. Through fresh waves of nausea and panic, he concentrated on sucking in air through his nose — slowing his heart beat and settling his stomach again.

Beneath him, the floor was hard and uneven, the corrugated steel of the back of the police truck. His vision swam slowly into focus, and through a flapping corner of the tarpaulin the dying embers of the school cast a dull glow on a large group of people with Butcher in the middle of them.

why did he take him away

In the back of Jamie's mind the girl screamed — a sudden, long, piercing cry of agony and distress that seared into his soul, until he felt that he might explode from the pain.

Then he passed out again.

What does that mean?

The four-wheel drive roared along the dirt road. Spotlights mounted on the front bullbar picked out the undulations and potholes, small puddles of liquid blackness framed against the stark red dirt. Occasionally a kangaroo would find itself caught in the rushing cone of light, and would stare into the headlights, transfixed for a couple of seconds, before leaping away into the blackness. In the cage Jamie slowly returned to consciousness, his head pounding. The back of the truck was slick with fine road dust thrown up by the tyres and sucked in by the vacuum that formed behind the speeding vehicle. Every bump and corrugation in the road launched him in a new direction. The gag had been removed and his legs untied, and he tried to sit up and brace himself against the side, but his hands were still cuffed behind his back, making it almost impossible to move against the momentum of the truck.

Through the pain and confusion, another emotion burrowed its way in. Fear. Real fear. For the first time in his life

140 ▲

Jamie knew the desperation of the trapped. Sweat broke out on the palms of his hands and down the back of his neck. In the dark chaos of the lurching police truck, his skin prickled and the fine hairs along his arms stood on end. This is what it feels like to be completely at the mercy of someone else.

A particularly big pothole threw Jamie into the air, crashing him back down onto the metal floor. The breath rushed out of him, leaving him prone and gasping. After a few more seconds, mercifully, he passed out again.

☐ where are they now?

"Wakey Wakey!" A hand reached into the cage and grabbed roughly at Jamie's collar, dragging him towards the door. He tried to get his footing, to roll over and steady himself, but he was pulled through the door and was unable to prevent himself crashing down onto the hard sand behind the truck.

"Get up."

Butcher stood over him, grinning. Jamie tried to climb to his feet but his hands were still bound, so Butcher grabbed his shirtfront and yanked him upright. His legs buckled under him and he staggered a little. A warm rush surged in his throat and he bent over, retching onto the ground at Butcher's feet.

"Charming," said the cop. "Not quite so cocky now, are we?"

Jamie was completely disoriented. It was still dark and the landscape remained cloaked. Off to one side though, the red scar of approaching dawn glowed in the sky. In the other direction the moon slunk towards the horizon. A couple of low buildings crouched to their left, indistinct but for their angular lines in the dim light.

"Welcome to Flaherety's Curse." ☐ Prison?

Butcher leaned in to Jamie's face.

"Hope you like it here, 'cause you're gonna be staying a while. Come on."

Grabbing a handful of Jamie's hair he started towards the

closest of the two buildings with Jamie trailing behind him, half dragged, half staggering. There was no door hanging in the frame and inside the room was almost bare. To one side some shapes suggested a couple of abandoned desks and other bits of disused furniture and rubbish piled haphazardly. In the middle of the room a single steel pole rose through the floor, supporting the ceiling.

"Now, I'm going to undo these handcuffs for a second. You're going to put your arms either side of the pole, and then I'll do them up again. Okay? If you're thinking of running, or even just refusing to behave, keep in mind that I can open and close the cuffs with one hand."

Reaching into his pocket with his left hand Butcher removed a key. With his right, he unholstered his pistol. The click of the safety catch being flicked off echoed against the bare walls. Butcher pressed the barrel into Jamie's temple so that the cold, hard circle of steel left an impression on his skin.

"One wrong move, son, and your brains are all over that wall. Now, let's see how good you can be."

Another faint click and the pressure on Jamie's left wrist eased. Having no choice, he wrapped his arms around the pole and seconds later the handcuff snapped back into place. Butcher squeezed it until the metal band cut into his flesh, making his eyes water.

"There now. That wasn't too hard."

Stepping back, Butcher surveyed his work. Jamie stood with one hand locked either side of the steel pole.

"I'd say you're not going anywhere for a while. This place is an abandoned mine office, just in case you're wondering and when I say abandoned, I mean it; no one ever comes here and you're in the middle of bloody nowhere, so even if you chew an arm off or something, you'll die of thirst before you find a town."

Butcher turned to leave. Jamie felt a wave of hopelessness

and despair gathering itself around him. He had to fight it. Somehow.

"Hey, Butcher."

The cop stopped in the doorway.

"You know this won't work, don't you."

Butcher laughed.

"See, that's where you're wrong. It will work, and I have got away with it. You don't think you're the first resident of Flaherety's Curse, do you?"

Jamie stayed silent.

"In a few days you'll be just another kid from the city who couldn't hack it in Port Barren. Burnt the school down, took off into the desert and died. We'll probably have a bit of a look around for you later today — don't think we'll find anything though." — Will someone save him?

He chuckled at his joke.

"Lorraine won't believe you."

"I wouldn't be counting on that if I was you, son. Lorraine knows which side her bread's buttered on. She'll believe whatever I tell her."

"Bullshit. She already knows about what you did to that girl. I told her." It was a lie, a desperate one, and Butcher knew it. He grinned.

"Let me tell you a little story about Lorraine, eh?"

Jamie glared sullenly.

"Few years back we had another young kid, much like yourself, sent up here. I think I mentioned him to you one time. Problem was that, just like you, this kid didn't have the brains to stay out of the way. Kept making a nuisance of himself. That was a worry, of course, but nothing that couldn't have been handled with some firm words from his parole officer, and that was where we had real problems. Silly bloody Lorraine got herself involved with the lad, if you know what I mean. Not sure why she did it exactly, it's not like men are thin on the ground in Port Barren or anything, is it? Bloody

Jamie isn't like that

▲ 143

stupid. Twice his age, and his parole officer, and that's what she goes and does. So of course he thought he'd be able to get away with pretty near anything."

Jamie stared in disbelief.

"It would have raised a hell of a stink if anyone'd found out about the affair. Lucky for Lorraine, no one did. Apart from me, that is." — *lorrainne was blackmailed* 🙂

Butcher stopped and looked expectantly at Jamie, obviously wanting a response. But Jamie stayed silent, letting the cop boast.

"Bit like yourself really, the dumb little bugger didn't know when to hold his tongue. Told me all about him and Lorraine one evening when I was having a little 'chat' with him about his future. Funnily enough, that same night the poor boy disappeared. Much like you're about to. Call it a favour to a friend if you like, but you can take my word for it — I made damn sure Lorraine knew all about what happened to that lad, and she never did a thing. It solved a lot of problems for her, so she didn't even try to help him. Just like she won't lift a finger for you. You're stuffed, mate. *What a bunch of croons*

Butcher took a couple more steps out the door, and then turned back again.

"You know the funny part? If you'd kept your mouth shut back in town I would have just arrested you for burning the school down and sent you off to prison for ten years. But you had to tell me how clever you'd been, didn't you? All about your little bit of detective work. I can't work out who was more stupid, you or McPherson, the dumb bastard."

He left. Jamie listened to the four-wheel drive roar into life and grind off along the dirt road.

TWENTY

The sound of the Toyota faded into the distance, and panic had taken hold of him again. The bleak pre-dawn light seeped through the broken windows revealing a bare floor, a couple of overturned desks and a bundle of rags strewn in one corner. Sand had found its way in through the broken windows and empty door frame. It coated everything in a dirty layer that had obviously sat undisturbed for years.

Jamie wanted to vomit again. His stomach churned, he doubled over and retched, but there was nothing left to come up. Eventually he took a few deep breaths and tried to calm down. *he could chew his arms off FP*

Gently easing himself to the floor, Jamie sat with his arms wrapped around the pole. He tried to lever his weight backwards against the handcuffs, but his pulling only caused the metal to bite harder into the flesh of his arms. His mind still clouded, he put more and more pressure against the unyielding steel bands, until finally the pain bit through his fear. Eventually the waves of panic gave way to a cold despair. Resting his head against the pole he tried to make himself relax and think.

The girl spoke to him again. The same disembodied voice, the words meaningless and foreign. This time however, Jamie heard more than just the words. Trapped in the hut in the middle of the desert, he was struck by the despair and the pain that formed the undercurrent to what she was telling him. His own situation, trapped, desperate and scared, was so similar to hers that he understood exactly what she was saying, even through the barrier of language. She was sharing his pain, as he was sharing hers. *Will he become another spirit*

Outside, the light grew stronger as the sun rose to fill the sky. Gradually, the early morning rustling and snuffling of animals feeding in the cool dawn faded into the eerie stillness of the midday desert.

He was wracked with thirst. He hadn't had anything to drink since he left the kitchen in Archie's place over twenty-four hours ago. His mouth and throat were dry and parched, his body felt numb and his head spun. Jamie knew that his body would soon wither in the desert heat. He hadn't eaten in ages, but it was the thirst that dominated his thoughts, constant and nagging, the craving for moisture so powerful that he began to lick his arms, trying to save the tiniest droplets of sweat from running off him.

It seems very wordy

Minutes passed like hours, and hours like days. Above his left temple his head throbbed where Butcher had struck him. He managed to lie down after a fashion, by twisting his body sideways around the pole and resting his head on one arm. It wasn't particularly comfortable, but he was exhausted and sleep came almost as soon as he closed his eyes.

Jamie dreamed. Visions and feelings swept through his subconscious. Images from childhood, his family, his parents, and Eddie. Always Eddie. In his dreams he returned again and again to that sterile prison visiting room, with Eddie telling him that as soon as he got out they'd do something straight; that Eddie would come and find him. Jamie knew that not even his brother would be able to come for him out here, and in his sleep his body trembled.

Mixed in with these were the more recent dreams. The

146 ▲

boat, Lorraine, Butcher, flames engulfing the school. Now and again he'd hear the voice. Not the scared, panic-driven voice, but something soft, soothing, gentle and reassuring. The words were incomprehensible but the meaning clear — "Don't be scared. Everything will be all right." The words of Archie's story rang in his ears:

> *The people must wait for another to come. A wanderer or a lost one* [is]
> *who can balance the pain. Can restore the land. Can bring the peace.* [he going to bring the peace]

Jamie slowly returned to consciousness. He felt as though Archie himself was there in the hut with him, retelling the story.

"Who am I?" The words formed themselves on Jamie's [peace] parched lips. "Am I a wanderer, or a lost one?" In his dazed state the question made less sense than ever, the answer, if there was one, remaining hidden behind a veil of pain.

He slid upright. This proved difficult. His arm had gone to sleep beneath the weight of his head, and his body was stiff and bruised from the brutal ride in the back of the truck. He rested his head on the pole and prodded cautiously at the lump on his temple.

By mid-afternoon the thirst was unbearable. The heat was worse than anything he had ever imagined. Constant rivers of precious moisture ran off him, soaking his clothes. Through the empty doorframe he could see a rectangular patch of horizon. Nothing but scrub and spinifex and the occasional rocky outcrop in the distance. No sound except the buzzing of a couple of bush flies that had found their way inside and hovered, unharassed, around Jamie's limp form.

Late in the afternoon a breeze came up, but it served only to stir the warm air inside the hut.

Early evening brought slow relief. As the sun eased towards the horizon, the temperature and stifling atmosphere in the hut began to abate slightly. The coolness revived him a little. Outside, the usual cacophony of insects greeting the approaching night was chirping into life. Jamie tried to settle

[What does that mean?]

again on the floor, hoping for the mercy of sleep, but his body was restless and twitchy. The urge to pull further at the handcuffs, to tear his body away from the pole, was overwhelming, but he fought against it. His wrists were already raw from the constant chaffing of the steel bracelets and he needed to conserve all the energy he could.

Someone began to sing. The sound floated around the hut, echoing off the bare walls. Jamie listened, fascinated, to tunes he vaguely remembered from his childhood. Nursery rhymes his mother used to sing to him. It was some minutes before he realised that the music was coming from his own mouth.

The worst part of it was the feeling of being hopelessly trapped, a total prisoner. Is this how Eddie must feel? he wondered. Waking up every day, caged, alone. The only thing that seemed important to Jamie now was freedom. He longed to rip himself away from the pole, to run from the hut out into the endless desert.

The thought of flight had firmly lodged itself in his brain. It took control of him and through a red haze he hauled himself up and started to tear at the pole. In his detached state he felt the skin sliding away from the muscle beneath, but the pain seemed somehow distant, as though it was happening to someone else. Again and again he wrenched his arms back until the chain of the handcuffs snapped up hard against the unyielding steel of the support beam. His hands and wrists grew raw as the layers of skin beneath the bracelets peeled away, the tiny trickle of blood mixing with the sweat that poured down his arms. Finally a bursting jolt of pain snapped him out of his madness, and he slumped to the floor.

He knelt with his head against the pole and let the tears of pain, frustration and despair run down his face. Outside, the symphony of insects suddenly stopped, and from out of the unexpected stillness the noise of an approaching engine carried clearly through the evening air.

TWENTY-ONE

At first Jamie thought that he must have been hallucinating again. The sound was so far off that it seemed no more real than the voice of the girl inside his head. He kept expecting to wake up, or for the engine noise to recede back into his dreams. Minutes passed, however, and the noise continued to grow louder and stronger until it stopped somewhere outside the hut.

"Jamie!" A voice. Familiar. *Rescuer?*

"In here." He tried to call but his throat was parched, and his voice, which just a few minutes earlier had been singing, suddenly refused to work. All he could manage was the barest of squeaks. For a couple of confused moments he almost laughed at the situation.

Footsteps crunching across the dirt towards the hut.

"Jamie?" A figure appeared in the doorway. Cameron started towards him then took in the scene. Saw the handcuffs, saw the blood, saw the exhaustion on his friend's face.

"Hang on, I'll be back." He sprinted from the room and Jamie's thirst-addled mind had a momentary panic attack, thinking that for some reason his rescuer was leaving again. But minutes later Cameron returned, a backpack and toolbox in hand.

*Hes saved!!!!! *

"Here." He pulled a bottle from a pocket on the side of the pack and held it to Jamie's lips. The bitter, metallic water of Port Barren had never tasted so good. Jamie gulped greedily, spilling it over his chin and neck.

"Steady." Cameron pulled the bottle back. "I've got plenty. Take it easy or you'll make yourself sick."

He let Jamie drink slowly for another minute and then put the bottle down.

"We'd better get you off that pole."

"How'd you find me?" Lubricated by the water, Jamie's voice returned, gravelly and scratchy.

"Later. We've got to get moving."

He dug around in the toolbox, pulled out a hacksaw and went to work on the chain.

"How'd you know to bring that?"

"Dad's a mining engineer — our car's full of tools."

"You can drive?"

"Since I was fourteen."

"And your dad lets you use the car?"

Cameron paused in his sawing for a second and gave Jamie a strained grin.

"That's why we're in a hurry. He doesn't know I've got it."

"Eh?" *very lucky*

"Actually, he's probably worked it out by now. It's a long story. I'll explain on the way back."

The steel chain was tough and unyielding. As the blade scraped back and forth, the grinding rasp of serrated teeth chewing through metal reverberated around the room. For fifteen minutes Cameron hacked away, and rapidly worked up a huge sweat. Droplets were running down his arms, onto the handle of the saw, making it difficult to control.

"Sorry," Cameron grunted, as the blade twisted unexpectedly and nipped at Jamie's forearm.

"It's okay. Can I have another drink?"

Cameron brought the water bottle to Jamie's lips for a sip

and then returned to the sawing. There was little conversation.

Finally the link parted and Jamie was free of the pole. Cameron helped him stand, and supported him as he tottered on unsteady legs.

"Come on!" Throwing the hacksaw into the toolbox, Cameron headed for the door, with Jamie hobbling awkwardly after him. They'd only gone a few paces when Cameron froze.

"Damn!"

"What?"

"Listen."

uh-o

Sure enough, in the distance Jamie could hear a familiar sound — an engine coming along the track towards the mine.

"How long have we got?" asked Cameron.

"Eh?"

"Until they get here — how much time?"

"Dunno."

"Well, how long was it between when you first heard me and when I pulled up outside?"

Jamie tried to think. His mind was working better now, refreshed by the water and by being able to move freely again, but his memory of the events of the day was fuzzy. Things that had happened just a few minutes ago were a little like the desert landscape — somehow distant and near at the same time. did he have another heat stroke?

"I'm not sure. I guess about ... three minutes?" It was a wild guess and Cameron knew it.

"Wait here."

Dropping the tool box and backpack, Cameron sprinted to a green Land Rover parked a few metres away. Flinging open the back, he grabbed a small bag and a plastic jerry-can of water which he heaved out onto the sand.

"Get that gear!" he shouted, nodding towards the equipment he had dropped earlier. As though in a dream, Jamie obeyed.

"Come on! Into the bushes."

Cameron led them straight towards the scrub at the edge of the mine-site clearing. Crashing through, they ducked down into the thorny plants.

"Cameron?"

"Yeah?" His voice was a whisper.

"Why don't we just wait and see who it is? It could be someone coming to help." — its butcher!?

Cameron turned to face him.

"I doubt it. I can guess who it is."

"Who?"

"Who do you reckon my dad's going to call on for help when he finds out the car's gone?"

There was no need to answer, because at that moment the approaching vehicle rounded the final bend and cruised into the parking area.

"Damn!"

Both boys went dead still. Cameron's guess had been right. It was Butcher, back in the police truck.

Jamie felt a sinking feeling return to his belly.

Leaving the engine running, the cop leapt from the driver's seat and ran across to the hut. Jamie was again surprised at the speed with which the large man moved. The two boys stayed motionless in their hiding place and watched as Butcher disappeared inside. In a couple of seconds he reappeared, but now there was no rushing and no panic. He walked calmly across to the waiting truck and switched off the engine. The diesel spluttered into an eerie silence. Taking a few steps away from the Toyota, Butcher stood and turned a slow circle, surveying every centimetre of scrub.

"Don't even twitch!" Cameron's whispered warning was pointless — Jamie was paralysed. I would be too!

Butcher finished his scan and turned his attention to Cameron's car.

"Oh, shit!"

"What?"

"The keys, I left them in the ignition."

Butcher climbed in and started up the Land Rover. He drove it slowly round the clearing then floored it straight towards the second mining hut.

The rotted asbestos wall gave way easily beneath the car's bullbar and a second later the Landie was parked inside, neatly hidden from any aerial search. The small cloud of dust that hung in the air where the car had crashed through slowly began to settle, but there was no sign of the cop.

who - cave? "Do you reckon he mighta hurt himself?" The question was whispered hopefully, but before Cameron had time to answer, Butcher emerged from the wrecked hut, a bundle of cables in his hand. To Jamie's alarm, he walked towards the edge of the scrub. Not right towards them, but pretty close. They held their breath.

The cop stopped, reached into his pocket and retrieved Cameron's car keys. Grinning, he drew his arm back and hurled them as far as he could into the scrub. Cameron twisted, trying to see where the keys might land, but they vanished into the gathering twilight.

Butcher stood for a few more seconds, still and silent, like a snake poised to strike, and then he yelled into the vastness.

"I know you can hear me, boys. Just thought you should know that, even if you do find the keys, they're no use to you without these." He held up the bundle of cables and sockets.

"Tell you what, how about you both come out now and we'll all head back to Port Barren together. No questions asked, no harm done? Eh?" *That's a lie*

His offer was met with heavy silence. Even the cicadas seemed to have gone quiet.

"Fair enough. Can't say I blame you. Still, worth a try."

At last he strolled across to his own vehicle.

"See you, fellas. Have a nice time."

Two minutes later only the settling dust cloud was left to remind the boys of his presence.

There in trouble

TWENTY-TWO

"Oh, man."

whats that?

They lugged the jerry-can between them towards the hut.

"What do we do?"

"First we get all this gear inside, then we fix your wrists up, then we think."

The water container was heavy. Jamie couldn't imagine how Cameron had managed to carry the thing all the way across to the bushes on his own, but he guessed that panic helped. *— They're lucky they saved it*

Once they'd set it down inside the hut, Cameron handed Jamie the hacksaw.

"You might as well work at trying to get those bracelets off, then I can bandage you up properly."

"Yeah, all right."

Holding the saw awkwardly, Jamie began to rasp the blade across the bracelet still attached to his left wrist. The tool was big and unwieldy, though, and kept turning in his hand. Cameron watched for a few seconds,

"Hang on a minute. Give it here." He started to fiddle with a couple of butterfly screws on the handle.

"It'll probably be easier with just the blade."

Sure enough, without the bulky steel handle Jamie found

it relatively simple to saw away at the remains of the hand-cuffs.

"While you're doing that I'm going to go and check the car. See if I can find anything useful."

"Useful?"

"My dad's a survival freak. He's got all sorts of gear in the back of that car. Like the water."

Jamie watched Cameron walk through the door, he had to stifle the urge to yell after him, to call him back. He didn't want to be alone in the hut. He went and sat on the hard sand out front. In the west, the last rays of the sun were sinking below the horizon, staining the sky a deep purple. Around him, the desert was slowly coming to life. The now familiar scrapes and rustles were almost reassuring. He kept sawing.

The bracelets were a much tougher proposition than the chain had been. The steel seemed harder, less malleable. Every now and then the blade would slip in his sweating palms and nick his arm or wrist. When this happened, he jumped a little but gave no real sign of pain.

Jamie went back inside for a drink and was picking up the small water container when a beam of torchlight flashed into the room from behind him. For the briefest of seconds Jamie felt a small flicker of hope. He spun around. Cameron was there, holding the torch.

"I knew dad had this hidden away in the back somewhere."

"Cool." Jamie tried to hide his disappointment.

"I found these as well." A couple of plastic water canteens knocked together in his other hand.

"Have we got any food?" With his thirst slowly becoming satisfied, a throbbing ache in his belly reminded Jamie that it had been a long time since his last meal.

"Yeah, quite a bit of dehydrated stuff, noodles and that sort of thing, some muesli bars, and a bit of fruit which I grabbed on my way out of the house."

"How about a bite to eat, then."

"No worries."

Cameron disappeared outside and returned with a couple of apples and a bar of chocolate.

"Here you go. Will that do?"

"Yeah. Thanks."

Gnawing hungrily at the fruit, Jamie felt he'd never experienced anything as good as the trickle of sweet juice running across his dry tongue and down the back of his throat.

"I've been thinking," said Cameron. "I reckon our best bet is to lie up here for a bit, give you a chance to recover slightly, then to hit out north across the desert towards town. I figure we can make it if we're careful." ⟵ what if butcher waiting for them

The plan sounded dubious to Jamie. He'd already experienced one day out here, and he wasn't keen for another. He didn't voice his concerns, though. Cameron sounded pretty confident. He seemed to know what he was doing.

"There's enough water in the jerry-can for the two of us for a few days, if we're careful."

"We can't lug that can through the desert, mate. We barely managed to drag it across the clearing."

"Yeah, but if we lie up for a day while you recover a bit, keep drinking and fill up the canteens, then we'll empty about half of it. I think we can jury-rig some sort of a harness or sled to drag it with us." ☐ how far out in the desert can they be?

"Shouldn't we just head back up the road?" That seemed to be the more sensible option. He'd heard stories of people breaking down in the desert, wandering away from their cars and never being seen or heard of again.

"Too far. Here, look."

Crouching, Cameron traced a series of lines in the sand with his finger — a rough map.

"Here's Port Barren, and this is the coast. We're about here. It's a great big loop to go by road from here back to town. It's about a hundred kilometres to the main highway and then another fifty or sixty into Port Barren. I'm not too sure but I figure that straight overland it's probably only forty or fifty kilometres. Two days walk."

"I dunno ..." Jamie remembered his night meandering between the patches of scrub just outside the town.

"Trust me, we'll never make the distance if we go back up the road. We'll run out of water for sure. And if we don't go, we'll die here — no question about that. If Butcher hadn't driven over the track when he brought you out here, then there's no way I'd have found you; it was touch and go a couple of times. No one ever comes here, so our best chance is to head straight towards town."

"Whatever. We can decide tomorrow anyway." *They're gonna get lost*

"Fair enough. How you going with the handcuffs?"

Jamie showed Cameron his progress. He was about a third of the way through the first bracelet.

"It's a bit harder than the chain."

"Yeah. Let me have a go."

"It's nicer outside."

Sitting on the sand in front of the hut, Cameron used the torch to study what Jamie had done, then put the blade in the right place and got to work. There wasn't the urgency of the previous occasion and it was easier having someone else do the cutting — the blade didn't slip around nearly so much.

"So how'd you know to look out here?" The question had been eating at Jamie and this was really the first chance he'd had to ask it.

"You'll never guess."

"Try me."

"Robb."

"Eh?"

"Constable Robb. The cop." *I knew he was a good guy!*

"How'd he know?"

"He didn't. Not exactly."

"What?"

"I'll have to explain from the start."

"Go on then."

"When the school went up, all hell broke loose. By the time they got the fire truck out of its garage the whole place was just about burnt to the ground. In the end, they didn't even bother hosing it down, just stood around and watched it burn itself out. After that, there were people everywhere. Butcher hung around for a while, ordering people about, and then he told the whole town to go back to bed. Most people did, but after Butcher had left there were still a few blokes, miners mainly, standing around the school getting themselves worked up. Everyone thought you'd done it, and a mob went around to Archie's place to get you, but he wouldn't let them in." *there were to be a lot of people that went to help Jamie*

"Archie?" Jamie found it hard to imagine the old man, whose door was always left open, refusing entry to anyone.

"Yeah. He stood out on his front verandah, with the door locked behind him, and told them that the only ones getting inside were Lorraine and Robb. That settled it as far as the town was concerned. You'd done it. It got pretty nasty. They stood around arguing for ages, and then a few of them went off to look for Butcher again, but he was nowhere to be found all of a sudden. So they dragged Robb back out of bed and made him go and talk to Archie."

"What about Lorraine?"

"A couple of people thought that they'd seen her around. Her car was still parked out in front of admin, but she wasn't inside, and nobody could find her. In the end it didn't matter. Robb went into the house and Archie told him that he hadn't seen you since yesterday morning. The crowd outside went nuts when they found out. A few of the rednecks suggested that Archie was hiding you, and it was getting pretty ugly. Four or five of the mining blokes were threatening to kick Archie's front door down, and Robb had his gun drawn, when Butcher turned up again out of the blue." *When he got back from dropping off Jamie*

"When was that?"

159

Cameron thought for a minute.

"This morning. At about eight, I guess."

"What did he do?"

"When they told him that they thought Archie had you stashed inside the house he laughed at them. 'Nah, Archie's a good bloke. If he says the little bugger's not in there, then he's not. More than likely he's gone bush.' There was still a bit of mumbling and muttering, but Butcher stood on the verandah of Archie's place and told everyone to clear off. Said there'd be a town meeting in front of admin at three this afternoon to discuss what to do about you and the school."

"And they went?" *I would be mad too*

"Yeah. There were still a few unhappy ones, but they all headed home. I was hanging about, waiting to see if I could nip around to the back of the house and see if you really were inside."

"You didn't believe Archie?"

Cameron stopped sawing.

"I just wanted to see for myself."

There was a strange note of defensiveness in Cameron's voice.

"I didn't get a chance, though. Butcher drove off to look for Lorraine and left Robb standing guard out the front of Archie's place, "in case any of the lads, or someone else for that matter, decides to come back". There was no way to sneak past Robb, so I was leaving when he spotted me and called me over. When I wandered across, he looks around, checking to make sure that no one's watching or listening, and he says, 'That was you with him in the boat that afternoon, eh?' I thought he was trying to tie me in with the school fire, but I couldn't really deny it, could I? So I nodded, figuring that there wasn't a lot he could prove anyway. And then he leans in close and says, 'Your mate's in big trouble. You know that?' I misunderstood what he was telling me."

"What d'ya mean misunderstood?" *Jim composed*

160.▲

"I thought he was having a go at me, so I got a little bit nasty, told him they couldn't prove you'd lit the fire. Though I've got to admit that with you disappearing and all I was beginning to wonder."

"Thanks, mate." Jamie's face grew dark at the suggestion.

"Well, put yourself in my position. School catches fire in the middle of the night and you haven't been seen for a whole day? It's surprising that I didn't just believe you were guilty straightaway, like the rest of the town." *I would*

"What happened then?" *Suspect Jamie too*

"Now it gets interesting. Robb shakes his head. 'That's not what I mean,' he says, 'You remember a coupla weeks ago, the admin windows? That wasn't your mate either. I know. I was watchin'."

Watching. A shiver ran down Jamie's spine. He remembered the solitary figure standing on the verandah of the admin building.

"Who was it then? I asked. 'The Sarge,' he says. I didn't believe him at first, but he explained. Butcher won't let him smoke when he's in uniform, which is basically all day, so he goes for a stroll late at night and has a couple of cigarettes. He was doing this when he saw Butcher smashing the windows." *※ – I knew Butcher the whole time!*

"Why didn't he say anything?"

Cameron shrugged. "I didn't ask. He probably would have, who knows, but he's only a constable, and he's got his job to think of. I got you off that one anyway, so there was no harm done and no need for him to annoy Butcher. I don't blame him."

"But how did he know I was out here?"

"He didn't."

"I thought you said …"

The left bracelet of the handcuff came away from Jamie's wrist. He massaged it gently.

"Shit, that feels better."

Cameron shone the torch on it. The skin was torn where the steel band had been pressed into it. The edges of the wound blazed an angry, inflamed red.

"I'd better get the first aid kit from the car and do something with that."

"Do the other one first."

"You're the boss." Cameron used the torch to position the blade against the right cuff.

"So, what happened then?"

"Lorraine showed up."

"Eh?"

"She came tearing up in that old bomb of hers, screeched to a stop in front of the house and leapt out. She said she'd just heard the news, and asked me if I knew where you were. I told her I didn't, and then out of nowhere Robb chimes in, "Wherever he is, he isn't close." That made Lorraine go quiet. She took on this really strange expression, like she'd forgotten that Robb and I were standing there watching her."

[handwritten annotation: old car — synonym, pointing to "old bomb" which is circled]

"What sort of expression?" Jamie remembered the unguarded moment when he'd asked her about the other missing boy.

"Almost angry. She looked majorly upset about something. Then she remembered where she was. 'What do you mean by that?' she asked Robb, and he gave her this look. Really weird, it was. Then he explained. 'The mileage on the truck. I checked it while the Sarge was talkin' to everyone. It's done a couple of hundred kilometres since I filled it up yesterday.' Lorraine went pale when he said that. I mean dead white. I thought she was going to faint. She whispered something."

Cameron paused, seeming to gather his thoughts.

"What?"

"I don't even know if she realised that she'd said it, she was so quiet, but I was close enough to hear. 'Flaherety's Curse', she said, then she rushed inside Archie's."

[handwritten annotation: was / Lorraine in on it?]

Cameron sawed in silence while Jamie digested all of this

information. It seemed to make sense. If what Butcher had told him was true, then Lorraine must have known where he was. *very lucky guy*

"How'd you find out about this place, then?"

"I thought it sounded like a mine. Dad's always going out to places with names like 'Doubtful Ridge' or 'Tucker's Revenge', so I ran home and checked his company map. I had to look pretty hard, but sure enough there it was, Flaherety's Curse, sixty kilometres west along the highway, turn left, and then it's about a hundred kilometres along unsealed tracks. First you head dead south for forty k's inland, and then the track gradually winds to the east, back towards Port Barren. This place was abandoned in the eighties."

"And you just took the car and left?"

"Not right away. Lorraine was still hovering around, so I followed her from Archie's place to the police station. She disappeared inside and after an hour I figured she wasn't coming to the rescue. I doubt her car would have made it anyway. Mum and Dad were still about, so I waited until they went off to the town meeting before I took the car."

"Won't you get busted?" *It would be worth it*

Cameron shrugged. "Dad'll be unhappy with me for a couple of days, but he'll come round, it being a mercy mission and all. I didn't count on Butcher trashing the car, though. We're just lucky that my old man is paranoid about desert survival."

"I'll say."

The silence was broken only by the grinding of the hacksaw against the steel bracelet.

"I reckon this blade's just about had it."

"How much have we got left?"

Jamie held the torch as Cameron sawed.

"Not much. Another ten minutes should do it."

From the bushes on the other side of the clearing, a shape

detached itself from the shadows and moved out into the open space.

"Cameron!"

"What?"

"Look —"

Jamie raised the torch and a startled kangaroo stared into the light for a couple of seconds before fleeing into the darkness. His dusty red coat left a blur in Jamie's vision.

"You see that!"

"Big one."

"Yeah. If he can get by out here we should be able to, eh?"

"Yeah." *What doesn't make any sence?*

A few more minutes of silence and then the other handcuff fell into the dirt.

"Thanks."

"Any time."

TWENTY-THREE

They spent the night in the back of the car. Their original plan was to settle down in the prefab where Jamie had been chained, but the cushioned back seats of the Land Rover looked more promising. . ⟶ •

As the sky began to lighten, Jamie woke and climbed out of the ruins of the mining hut leaving Cameron still asleep. He moved on legs that were stiff and sore and the wound on his head throbbed, but he felt a little better for a solid night's sleep. — ♀ I'll say

After a drink, he wandered to the far side of the clearing to relieve himself. The sun hadn't yet climbed above the horizon and in the cool pre-dawn light the desert was alive. About a hundred metres out a group of red kangaroos grazed in the scrub. The tracks of creatures that had crossed the clearing during the night dotted the soft earth.

The air was cool against his skin. Jamie took another sip from the canteen and stayed as still as possible, absorbing the power of the sunrise.

With the horizon growing lighter and the sky glowing a deep crimson, all of the fear and tension that had for weeks been dominating his thoughts seemed to evaporate, drawn out of him by the gentle morning breeze and blown away over the red sand and dusty plants. He'd been left out here to die and yet all he could feel was a sense of unbelievable oneness; of belonging. Jamie knew, right at the core of his being, that he was actually supposed to be there, was meant to be standing in that clearing drinking in the dawn. He understood in an instant the meaning of destiny.

At the second the sun broke the horizon, a flash of green lit the entire sky, just for an instant. It had come and gone almost before he'd had time to register it. Immediately the sun began its ascent into the heavens and the heat intensified.

"Pretty amazing." Cameron had come up from behind without Jamie hearing.

"Yeah. You see that flash?"

"What flash?"

"Just as the sun came up. Huge burst of green light."

"Sorry. Must have missed it."

"It was pretty quick. Drink?" Jamie offered the canteen.

"Thanks."

They stood watching silently for a few minutes as the kangaroos, their breakfast over, bounded off into the desert.

"Guess they're off to find somewhere shady for the day." Cameron drank deeply.

"Yeah."

"I've been thinking we should do the same thing."

Jamie looked at Cameron, puzzled. He'd thought that Cameron would have been keen to get started just as soon as it was light enough.

"We should stay here for the day, in the shade. Drink up as much water as we can and travel at night, when it's cooler. We've got the torch and the moon's full at the moment, so light shouldn't be a problem."

"What about direction? How do we find our way?" As far as Jamie was concerned, if the sun was up, then at least they'd know roughly where they were headed.

"There's a little compass in the dash of the car. I'll try and lever it out."

"Won't your dad mind?"

"He'd rather we got back alive."

Yesterday, the thought of walking off into the desert had terrified Jamie. Now, with that strange, almost intimate feeling of belonging still fresh in his memory, the idea of crossing the dry expanse had lost some of its fear. — he's in survival mode

"We oughta rest up, then."

"Yeah. We'll need to make twenty-five or thirty kilometres tonight and then find some shelter for tomorrow."

By now the sun had climbed fully above the horizon and already Jamie could feel its rays burning at his face and arms. An ache in his belly reminded him that it had been a long time since his apple and chocolate dinner.

"How about some breakfast?"

"Yeah, all right." Cameron seemed hesitant. "I guess we can have a cereal bar and a couple of apples, but we'll need to save a lot of what we have for the walk."

"Fair enough."

Inside the main hut they took stock of their provisions. Cameron had grabbed a box of eight muesli bars and half a dozen apples before he'd left. His dad's desert survival kit yielded a few packets of dried biscuits and concentrated food, which they decided to save.

"Have an apple."

They crunched at the fruit and the gnawing in Jamie's belly subsided.

"Want another?" — dont eat too much, or they'll run out

"Yeah, okay."

"I'm going over to have a crack at the compass before it gets too hot. You can try to rig up some sort of a harness to drag the water along with."

"Shouldn't we make a sled or somethin'?"

"I don't reckon we'll need it, it's just more work. That red

▲ 167

sand's pretty soft, and we should be able to pull the jerry-can through it."

"You're the boss."

It was true. Since Cameron had arrived he'd taken charge. Jamie had to admit that he seemed to be thinking pretty clearly. Taking a screwdriver and a couple of other tools from the toolbox Cameron headed back to the car. His confidence was reassuring. *he's a good friend*

Jamie turned his attention to the water-can. A moulded handle on the top behind the spout was the logical place to tie a harness. It was still heavy, even with a third of the water already drunk or in the canteens. What he needed was some rope.

He wandered over to the car, clambering through the wrecked wall into the cooler interior of the hut. The bulk of the four-wheel drive filled almost the entire room, leaving just enough space for Jamie to squeeze along one side. Cameron was already somewhere under the dashboard, making crunching noises.

"Your old man have any rope in here?"

"Don't know." Cameron's voice was muffled. "Have a look around."

There was nothing of any use in the back. Just lots of boxes of tools and instruments, most emblazoned with the Great Northern Mining Company logo. Under the floor of the boot however, he discovered a set of jumper leads and a towing rope. These looked promising. *What if butene comes back!?*

"Found something."

"Great." Cameron didn't stop what he was doing.

It took Jamie half an hour to rig a makeshift harness, using the blunt hacksaw blade and a pair of pliers to get the metal clips off the ends of the cables, and then putting together a sort of belt and shoulder strap which tied on to the handle. Dragging it all outside took a lot of effort. He eased the jerry-can onto a patch of soft sand near the side of the hut, careful not to allow the plastic container to drop too heavily onto the hard ground, then shrugged the harness into place.

A couple of steps and the jumper leads stretched a little, before drawing up hard against the heavy container. Jamie shifted his weight. It was an effort, but slowly he began to haul the water container through the sand.

"Cool!" He broke into a grin.

A few more steps, building momentum, and it became easier to pull the load, but the cables started to bite sharply into his waist and shoulders. *that would be a pain to carry*

"That's no good," he muttered. They'd be dragging it along for hours and the last thing they needed was to have the harness cutting into them.

Pulling the whole assembly back to the hut, Jamie wriggled out of the harness and untied it from the handle of the can. Back inside, he looked around for something to use to pad the shoulder and waist straps. A bundle of rags someone had cast into the far corner caught his attention.

Crossing the hut, a sudden, nervous tremble ran the length of his spine. The pleasant, connected feeling that had been lingering all morning vanished abruptly, and was replaced by a coldness, reminiscent of how he felt when he was in Port Barren. For a second he stopped, listening, searching for some cause of the uneasiness. The only noise, however, was the hammering from where Cameron was working in the other building. Trying to shrug the feeling off, he picked up one of the rags from the top of the bundle. Something rolled from under the pile and bumped against Jamie's foot. He looked down.

Lying on the floor staring back up at him with empty eyes was a human skull. *Why would it be in his car?!*

TWENTY-FOUR

"Who do you reckon it is?" Cameron stared at the bundle in the corner of the hut.

"I can take a guess." *— Oh, its notin the car*

"Who?"

"Have a look at this." Jamie offered him the rag, which he still held.

Cameron examined it, puzzled. It was an old blanket with faded blue and white stripes on it.

"I still don't get it."

"In the corner."

Cameron peered closely. Stitched into the fabric at the edge of the blanket were the initials GNMC.

"Great Northern Mining Company?"

"From the nursing station back in town."

"How do you know?"

"I've been there, remember?"

"So?"

"So, who else do we know spent the night there?"

Cameron stared at him, his face a mixture of surprise and dismay.

"You really think it's her?"

"Who else could it be?"

A feeling of release swept over Jamie. It wasn't a powerful emotion, not like the fear he'd experienced in the back of the police truck, or even the peacefulness of that morning. It was more gentle, like a sigh of relief. Cameron interrupted his reverie.

"I've got to go outside."

Cameron had gone pale, and looked shaken. Jamie followed him out and found him flopped down in the shade at the side of the hut.

"How'd she get out here?" ‑ Butcher should be in ⚹ Prison

"Same way I did."

An unsteady silence filled the atmosphere around them.

"At least the bastard didn't handcuff her."

"He wouldn't have needed to, would he? She was pretty crook."

Jamie went back inside and fetched a canteen. The other boy accepted it gratefully and took a long drink.

"Why didn't he bury her? Hide her or something?" Cameron asked.

"He wouldn't need to would he? You said yourself that it would have been impossible to find this place without fresh tracks to follow. No one comes here. Besides, Butcher's too arrogant."

"Arrogant?" ← Thinks he can get away with all of this

"Yeah. You should have heard some of the stuff he said when he dumped me here. It didn't even cross his mind for a second that he'd get caught."

Cameron was silent, considering. "So what do we do about her?"

"Do?"

"Yeah. Shouldn't we bury her or something?"

Jamie sat next to him, leaning back against the fibro wall.

"I think we should take her with us."

"What?"

"We can't leave her here. She doesn't want to stay."

Cameron gave Jamie a strange look.

"It's a skeleton. We can't carry it."

"Why not?"

"It's ..." Cameron stopped, unable to give voice to his thoughts. Jamie took the opportunity to drive his point home.

"Think about it, mate. If we bring her back, what've we got? We've got evidence against Butcher, that's what."

"Yeah but ..."

"Without her, then it's just our word against Butcher's, and you know what he's like. Hell, he's probably back there right now spinning some bullshit story to the town to make the two of us look like criminals. We need her. She needs us, too."

"What about the extra weight?" ~~But~~ its wormit *

"Look at what's left of her, just a few bones. That's nothin'."

They lapsed into silence. Jamie let Cameron think it through for himself. He wasn't ready to tell his friend that the girl had been talking to him, calling him.

"How do we carry her?"

"In the bag. There'll be room."

"You'll have to pack it. I'm still trying to get that compass out."

"Fair enough." Cameron still wasn't comfortable with the thought of bringing the girl across the desert with them, but at least he was coming around.

"Look at it this way. Perhaps she's been looking after us so far, eh? Maybe we owe her."

"Yeah, possibly." He didn't sound convinced. "I'm going to get back to the car before it gets hotter."

"Okay. I've got to finish the harness, then I'll get the bag packed."

Cameron took another long swig from the canteen then climbed to his feet.

"You really reckon we can pull this off?"

Jamie looked hard at him. For the first time, a glimmer of doubt lurked in the other boy's expression.

* 'They have a good thing goin here

"I don't see that we've got much choice."

Without another word Cameron padded off across the hot sand to continue his work. Jamie took himself back inside.

its gonna be an adventure

Desert

TWENTY-FIVE

The sun was dropping to the horizon when they set out. The compass in the central console of the Land Rover had proved immovable, and rather than waste another day Cameron decided they could risk the journey without it.

Jamie wore the backpack and Cameron had the water container harnessed to his shoulders. Looking out at the sunset the desert suddenly seemed even more immense — if that was possible. Cameron outlined his plan.

"It shouldn't be too hard. We'll take a bearing from where the sun sets. That'll be pretty much west. As long as we keep moving roughly north, we have to hit the highway eventually. Then we can hitch a ride back into town."

"I thought people in the desert wandered in circles?"

"I read how to beat that. We pick a landmark in the direction we want to head, and from there we pick another one further up the trail. Provided that we keep lining things up behind us, we should keep going in a straight line."

"You sure about this?" Jamie still couldn't shake the feeling that following the road would be safer.

"No. But I told you, I reckon it's our best chance."

Staring ahead, both contemplated the immensity of the desert. It extended away forever, lit by the diffused pink glow of sunset. An almost eerie stillness descended on the landscape. The scufflings and scrapings were momentarily hushed, almost as though the land itself was waiting for something to happen.

"Let's get on with it, then."

With a few tentative steps, Cameron took the weight of the water container and started to drag it forwards across the soft sand. It was a little less than half full and left a long, wide track in the soft earth.

"A friend always leaves a trail."

"Eh?" Cameron threw a puzzled look in Jamie's direction.

"I read that in the book we're studying for English at the moment. It's an old Aboriginal saying."

The evening was cool and the creatures of the desert were feeding. Everywhere they looked there were signs of activity. A clicking here, a stirring in the spinifex there. Not a breath of wind ruffled the bushes, as they walked in silence.

The afternoon had gone quickly. Cameron had stayed out of the hut as much as possible, preferring to continue his war with the dashboard. Jamie had finished the harness and packed for the walk. They needed to take the food, the first aid kit, the torch and, of course, the girl. He'd decided to wrap her up in the old blanket and to place her in the bottom of the pack, under the food, so they wouldn't need to disturb her again.

At first he'd been nervous at the prospect of handling a skeleton but his anxiety soon fell away. The bones were dry and bleached after so long in the desert air. He was reminded of the skeletal remains of the old boat. Gathering them together on the blanket, he stacked them neatly, careful not to leave anything behind, and then wrapped the faded blue and white cloth around them. He used another old piece of material to protect the skull. Jamie had weighed it in his hands for a couple of minutes, holding it with his arm extended and staring into the empty eyes. It seemed so fragile and delicate — as thin as eggshell — difficult to imagine as a living, breathing person. He wrapped it carefully and placed it in the backpack.

The pack was heavy, but it felt light on his back as Jamie walked beside Cameron out into the evening desert. There were three of them, not two, making their way out to face the ordeal of the desert. The girl's presence filled Jamie. She'd been watching him, helping him, calling him, ever since the moment he'd stepped off the bus and into Port Barren. Now, even though she was nothing more than a fragile pile of bones, Jamie was carrying her home. It was a thought from which he drew comfort.

As the sun touched the horizon, the desert seemed to grow cooler; a wave of darkness swept across it. Around them, the evening erupted into a joyous explosion of sound — clicks and buzzes. Again Jamie was picked up and carried by a feeling of belonging. Of oneness.

Cameron pointed at a finger of red rock that reached skywards, breaking the smooth curve of the horizon ahead of them.

"We'll head for that pinnacle out there. Should be able to see it pretty clearly, even in the dark."

The ancient stone glowed a fiery red in the last rays of sunset. In the gathering twilight it was hard to tell the distance to the pinnacle, but Jamie would have guessed it at two or three kilometres.

Behind them, the two huts of Flaherety's Curse were already fading into the gloom of the evening. To their left the dying sunset stained the horizon a bloody crimson. Jamie was pleased to be getting away from the close, tense atmosphere inside the huts. He thought of Cameron's theory about places absorbing positive and negative energy from the people inside them, and wondered about Flaherety's Curse. If Cameron was right, then what spirits had they left behind in those old prefabricated shacks, and what were they taking with them?

The night grew darker and stars appeared over the eastern horizon.

"How are you feeling?" Cameron didn't break step, but shot the question sideways as he trudged through ankle-deep sand.

"Okay. Pretty good actually. What about you?"

"This thing weighs a ton. It's gonna be a long night."

"We can swap if you want."

"No thanks. I'd rather ..." The sentence remained unfinished. Jamie knew what was on Cameron's mind.

"It's not all that bad, you know."

"What isn't?"

"Carrying her. It's not like you'd think."

"It's not that. I just ..."

"Listen," Jamie said. "You know that time you were talking about energy, places being haunted and that?"

"Yeah."

"Well, think of it that way. We're taking her away from one of those negative places. Releasing her, if you like. She'd be grateful."

"I guess."

The effort of dragging the water stopped the conversation, but Jamie could tell that Cameron was turning the idea over.

After an hour or so of walking, the rock pinnacle still seemed a long way off. They stopped for a drink and something to eat.

"Apples again?"

"Last two. They'll go off if we don't eat 'em."

The moon was yet to rise and the faint starlight cast an ethereal glow across the stark landscape. The apples were floury, but both boys were starving, so neither complained.

"How far off do you think that rock is?"

"Dunno. Hard to say."

"I think we're probably about halfway there."

Jamie thought they were a lot less, but decided not to argue the point.

"Let's keep movin' then."

They refilled their canteens, to lighten the load in the jerry-can. Jamie went to pick up the backpack, but Cameron stopped him.

"You mind swapping for a while?"

"No worries." Jamie grinned in the darkness.

They pressed on. The moon stayed below the horizon and their eyes slowly adapted. Even with the padding, the waist and shoulder straps of the harness bit deeply into Jamie's flesh. His legs soon ached from the constant strain of pulling the load through the soft sand. Gradually the pain spread from his calves into his thighs and lower back and up into his shoulders.

Cameron had obviously experienced the same thing during his time in the harness.

"If you want to take a break or anything, just say so. It's pretty heavy work."

Jamie managed a nod in reply, all his energy concentrated on the task of keeping his legs moving.

Progress was slow. Like the night Jamie had woken up in the desert and tried to get home, it proved impossible to travel in a straight line. They kept having to divert around thickets of spinifex and scrub. Several times they needed to carry the water can across dry creek beds that were littered with rocks and stones that would have punctured or cracked the brittle plastic. By midnight they were both exhausted. The rock peak still seemed a long way off.

"Bloody thing's not gettin' any closer." Jamie collapsed onto the sand.

"It is. Just slowly. It's bigger than we thought."

The moon had risen some time during the last couple of

hours. Jamie hadn't even noticed. He'd been concentrating so hard on putting aside the pain in his body.

"You think we'll get there tonight?"

"Yeah. I reckon in another hour or so."

Moonlight made their progress slightly faster. Small paths and trails between the bushes became easier to see. They spotted obstacles earlier and set their course to avoid them. At half past one they finally arrived at the base of the pinnacle.

"We'll take a longer break here, eh?"

"Yeah, good idea." Jamie shrugged off the harness and sat with relief on a nearby rock, examining the tower of stone that rose above them into the silver sky.

"Pretty amazing."

"Yeah."

The bottom of the pinnacle was littered with small boulders and rocks. Out of this the rough sides of the granite column climbed almost vertically, probably seventy or eighty metres into the night. Even in the moonlight, small fissures and cracks in the surface of the rock showed clearly.

"You reckon it's climbable?"

Jamie stared in disbelief.

"You're kiddin' me. You'll kill yourself."

"If I can get up there, even just a little way, I can probably pick our next navigation mark."

"You're doin' it on your own then, mate. I'm buggered."

"Yeah, fair enough. We'll swap loads again for the next bit."

Cameron walked up and down thoughtfully at the edge of the rocks.

"I reckon I can get at least a little way up."

"Just don't break your leg."

"I'll be careful."

Cameron's silhouette moved carefully over the scree that littered the base of the monolith, and slowly worked its way upwards and around the side of the rock, until it was hidden from view. Every now and then Jamie would flinch as a loose rock tumbled down the side and thumped into the sand. He was exhausted, almost too tired to think. He felt sleep starting to worm its way into his body.

"Jamie!" Cameron's voice floated down from somewhere in the darkness above him, waking him.

"Yeah?"

"Take the torch and go a few hundred metres back along the path, then shine it this way."

"How come?"

"I can't see the mine site, so I need something back that way to take a bearing from."

"Hang on."

Even the effort of climbing back to his feet was painful. How he was going to manage two or perhaps even three days of this was a mystery. Still, he dug around in the bag until he found the torch, trudged back along the trail left in the sand by the water can, and waved the torch towards the rock.

Cameron yelled something but the words were muffled by distance. Jamie held the torch for another minute or so before picking his way back to where they'd left the gear. Cameron was already down and refilling the canteens.

"There's a dark patch a few kilometres ahead that I think might be a clump of trees. It's in the right direction and we should be able to get there before sunrise, easily."

"Let's wait a bit longer first."

Cameron was clearly impatient to get moving again, but he agreed to sit for another ten minutes. The rock was still slightly warm from the day's sun and felt pleasant against Jamie's back. He closed his eyes. While they'd been walking he hadn't noticed how cool the evening had become.

"Don't fall asleep." Cameron's voice jolted him back into wakefulness.

"I wasn't."

"You ready?" Without waiting for an answer Cameron

leapt to his feet and started to secure himself into the harness. Jamie hauled himself up and hoisted the backpack onto aching shoulders.

The slow haul through the night seemed to stretch on forever. At about four the moon sank back below the horizon, and soon after the first hints of dawn appeared. Jamie was alarmed to see the horizon growing light almost directly ahead of them.

"We still on course, do you think?"

Cameron looked concerned, but tried to hide it.

"Yeah. This time of year the sun's moving further north."

He didn't say anything more, and Jamie's silence suggested that he'd accepted the explanation. In his mind, though, the feeling of belonging and peace had given way to a growing sense of doubt.

During the long hours of the early morning the scrub grew slightly less dense and it became easier to walk in a straight line towards their destination. For much of the hike they were able to travel two abreast. For reasons he couldn't explain, the gradual change in the landscape bothered Jamie.

By five the sky had lightened considerably and the clump of trees they were using as a guide was only about another kilometre away. Off in the distance behind them the pinnacle of rock glowed an iridescent red as the first rays of sunlight struck it. They stopped to look for a few seconds, and Cameron's gaze fell to the ground behind them.

"Shit!"

"What?"

"Look."

Stretching back towards the pinnacle, a dark smear in the sand marked their path.

"The water!"

Somewhere during the hours of the early morning, some-thing, a rock perhaps, had dragged against the side of the water container, splitting it open along the seam where the two halves were moulded together.

Both dived for the jerry can, but to their horror only about half a litre remained slopping around in the bottom. The rest had leaked out and soaked into the thirsty red sand.

"What do we do now?"

Cameron shook his head, fear now obvious in his eyes.

"Might as well get to the trees for a start."

They carried the container upside down between them, preserving the last few precious drops. It took about fifteen minutes to reach the shade.

From a distance, the trees had looked green and inviting. Up close they were nothing more than a scraggly bunch of sad-looking shrubs, slightly bigger than those in the desert around them. The boys collapsed onto the sand beneath them.

"Should we go back?"

"Where?"

"To the mine."

"And then what?"

Cameron was right. It made no sense to retrace their steps back to Flaherety's Curse. There was no water there, and no hope either.

"What do you suggest then?"

Cameron searched the surrounding horizon desperately.

"We rest up here for the day. Tonight we keep heading north. We should hit the highway sometime tomorrow morning."

"What about water?"

He shrugged. "We'll have to ration what we've got."

There didn't seem much else to say. Cameron settled himself in the deepest bit of shade he could find, and Jamie did the same.

TWENTY-SIX

The day wore on and the sun grew more and more intense. Jamie and Cameron lay in the shade and slept.

Cameron was the first to wake, late in the afternoon.

"Jamie!"

Slowly, reluctantly, Jamie came to. His body felt like it was on fire. Every muscle ached and his legs and arms were stiff.

"I feel like crap."

"Me too. At least you're not burned." During the day, Cameron's patch of shade had gradually disappeared, leaving him sleeping in the direct rays of the afternoon sun.

"Mate, you look like a light bulb."

"Thanks. I feel like one."

Jamie stood up, stretched some feeling into his numb limbs and shook the sand out of his hair and clothes.

"More sand inside my shirt than outside."

"Tell me about it."

"Pass the water."

"Don't have too much."

"She's right." They had decanted what little water was left into the canteens. Jamie took a small mouthful then handed it to Cameron, who did the same.

"Hungry?"

"Yeah."

"Here."

Jamie caught the muesli bar that flew his way.

"Thanks."

They munched for a few minutes, the dry cereal absorbing the little remaining moisture in Jamie's mouth. He longed for another drink, but wouldn't let himself ask.

"We should've had the drink second." Cameron's voice was muffled by the food.

"Yeah."

The small meal was enough to take the edge off their appetite but was hardly satisfying. Cameron, however, was already picking up the pack.

"It's late, we'd better get a move on."

"I'll take the bag first if you like. You're pretty burned."

"You sure?"

Jamie didn't answer. He took the bag from Cameron and shrugged it over his shoulders. Cameron looked to where the sun was dying in another spectacular display of red and orange light.

"Off that way, I'd say." He gestured in the general direction they'd been headed the night before. Ahead of them, the desert plain stretched featureless, except for the sparse patches of scrub.

"What'll we aim for?"

"There's nothing really out there."

"We'll just have to take a guess at it."

Cameron started out, but Jamie held back. It had been bad enough walking out into the desert from the mine site. Leaving the security of the trees with no fixed point to aim for made him even more nervous. He called after Cameron.

"Hey, Cam —"

"What?" Cameron sounded irritable and annoyed. Not like the easy-going guy Jamie had come to know.

"Nothin'. Don't worry about it."

That night seemed much longer than the previous one. With no visible destination in sight, it was harder to keep moving at a reasonable speed. At least before they'd had goals to achieve, some end to the drudgery of walking, and this had been a source of motivation. Now, trekking through the featureless plain, time seemed to crawl along.

When they stopped for rests there was no conversation. Each sat alone with his thoughts and pain. Not only had the landscape changed but the surface underfoot had altered too. The soft red sand slowly gave way to harder, rockier, gravel-like ground with less and less vegetation. The upside of this was that it became easier to walk, and without the load of the water container they moved much faster. In the early hours of the morning, as they sat by a small clump of bushes, Cameron broke the silence.

"At this rate we'll hit the highway later today for sure." Jamie detected a hint of the old optimism back in the other boy's voice.

Dawn approached bright and clear, with neither highway nor shelter in sight. They took a new bearing off the sunrise and altered their course a little. At eight o'clock Cameron stopped.

"What do you reckon?"

"We'd better find some shelter soon."

"Not a lot around."

They surveyed the landscape. The patches of bushes and vegetation were now so few that Jamie felt as though he were standing on the moon. Off to the right something grabbed his attention.

"What about over there?"

Perhaps a kilometre away something broke the smooth curve of the horizon. It was nothing more than an uneven patch of ground that might have been a small outcrop.

Cameron shrugged. "It's in the wrong direction."

"Can you see anything else around?"

Cameron shrugged again and started walking towards where Jamie had gestured.

Unlike the pinnacle, this feature was closer than it seemed. It wasn't much — just a few biggish boulders, strewn haphazardly.

"What do you think?"

"It'll have to do." Cameron dropped the pack and the two of them collapsed into the shade of the biggest rocks.

By ten-thirty what little shelter had been provided by the granite rocks had vanished altogether. For the middle few hours of the day they crouched near the rocks, exposed and vulnerable to the searing rays of the sun.

The harsh light burned at Jamie's flesh. He could feel himself absorbing the heat and starting to glow from within. The sand became increasingly uncomfortable, every grain scratching and scraping against skin made delicate from exposure. A little after two, he walked around to the other side of the rocks. Some shade was forming there, a tiny patch of darkness in the lee of the rock, growing as the sun began its slow descent towards the western horizon. He tried to stir Cameron.

"Cam, get up!"

Cameron mumbled something unintelligible. Grabbing his arm, Jamie tried to haul him to his feet. There was no way he could actually have managed to lift someone Cameron's size, let alone drag him around the boulder, but the tugging at his arm woke him a little, and Cameron slowly came to.

"I'm roasting."

"I'm not surprised."

Jamie was burnt, but Cameron, with his fair skin, was positively frying. His arms, face and legs glowed an angry red.

"Get around here. There's a bit of shade." He led Cameron to where the patch of shadow stood out a stark black against the red sand. In the glare of the sun, the protected shelter behind the rock appeared as a pool of darkness. In Jamie's fevered imagination, he almost pictured himself diving head-first into its cool depths. The moment passed, however, and they settled onto the sand. Despite the shade, it wasn't much cooler and the ground was hard beneath them.

"You reckon we can spare a sip of water?"

"Just a little."

They retrieved a canteen and each took a small mouthful. The water was warm, yet still ran like ice down the back of Jamie's throat. He could actually feel it sitting thick and heavy in his stomach.

"Want some more?"

Cameron thought about it.

"Yeah, why not? The highway can't be too far off now. We'll probably find it early tonight."

He took another mouthful, a long swig this time, from the water bottle. Jamie did the same and suddenly the canteen was empty.

"That's it."

"Really?"

"Look." Jamie turned the bottle upside down. Not even a drop fell from the spout.

"I thought we had more than that."

Jamie shrugged.

"What's left then?"

Jamie took the other canteen and shook it. The water sloshed around inside.

"It's about half full."

"Save it for tonight."

"Yeah."

The conversation stopped and Cameron fell asleep again. Sheltered now, he rested more comfortably. Jamie tried to nod off, but his mind kept churning over their problems — the change in the landscape, the increasing scarcity of plant life, their lack of water. Gradually, the old worries — Butcher, Lorraine, Archie and Robb — began dominating his thoughts.

He stared wide-eyed into the brightness of the afternoon, but eventually his chin dropped to his chest and he dozed, drifting into a dreamy, uncomfortable sleep. He was trapped in a circle of flames. The fires raged at his body and the girl stood just outside the circle, beckoning and calling softly to him in strange words. The ring of fire kept shrinking, drawing closer and closer to where he stood, paralysed. Finally, he made a running leap for the outstretched hand of the girl. The temperature scorched his body and he collapsed onto the ground. The girl was nowhere to be seen, but Butcher stood above him, nightstick in hand. "I told you to look out for me, son." He raised his arm, the club fell towards Jamie's head ...

"Jamie!" Cameron shook him into consciousness. "You right, mate?"

"What?" Jamie was groggy with sleep.

"You were whimpering and moaning something awful. I thought you were having a seizure."

Jamie sat up slowly and tried to throw off the lingering images of the dream.

"Nah. I'm right. Just a bad dream."

"Here." Cameron held the remaining canteen to Jamie's lips and without thinking Jamie took a couple of big mouthfuls.

"Hang on!"

"Shit! I'm sorry, Cam. I forgot, really. I ..."

Cameron shook the bottle. The splash of liquid inside sounded different now — more hollow, higher pitched.

"Doesn't matter. There's still a bit left."

Jamie felt terrible. He'd been so disoriented that it hadn't occurred to him that he was drinking so much.

"You have it mate, I ..."

"We'll save it for later." Cameron screwed the lid back on and slung the canteen around his neck. "You ready? We'd better get moving."

It was almost dark. They had slept much later than they'd intended. Jamie looked around.

"Which way?"

"This way, I think." The last stain of the sunset coloured the horizon ninety degrees from the direction Cameron indicated.

Cameron started but suddenly Jamie stopped.

"You okay?"

Jamie pinched the bridge of his nose between his thumb and forefinger, squeezing at the corners of his eyes. His head spun. The girl's voice was suddenly loud and insistent.

"We're goin' the wrong way."

"Eh?" Cameron looked at him strangely.

"We're heading in the wrong direction. I reckon we should be more over there."

"That's too far west. We'll end up going back the way we came."

"Nah. This way's takin' us further and further into the desert, mate. Look at the bushes."

"What about them?"

"There's barely any around now. Back at the mine there was scrub all over the place. I reckon we're headin' too far east."

A perplexed expression formed on Cameron's face, and he turned a couple of slow circles, examining the landscape carefully, before staring closely at Jamie. In the twilight Jamie could see the doubt in the other boy's face.

"You really think?"

So far Cameron had done all of the navigating, and his plan was a sound one, but it was impossible for Jamie to fight down the feeling that they needed to head more towards the sunset.

"It's just a feelin'. I'm probably wrong."

Cameron looked for a long time in both directions.

"Let's give it a try anyway. Nothing to lose."

They walked towards the sunset.

TWENTY-SEVEN

The water ran out just before dawn. Through the long night's hike they'd taken only the tiniest of sips, enough to simply wet their lips, but even so the last drops fell into Cameron's mouth as the glow of sunrise started to lighten the sky behind them.

"At least we've been going in a straight line."

Jamie didn't answer. They were following a wide, sandy trail through scrubland. The hard rocky ground had petered out a little after three o'clock, and they'd returned to slogging through the soft, deep sand. Both knew that without water this would be their last day of walking. Already they were badly dehydrated — another day like yesterday would finish them.

"We oughta look around for somewhere to rest up."

Jamie nodded, too tired to speak.

"At least there's more bushes and stuff now."

As the sky above them grew steadily lighter, an endless carpet of spinifex, scrub and sand was revealed. Ahead of them, somewhere in the distance, Jamie thought he heard birds calling, but put it down to imagination.

"Over there, eh?" Jamie followed the direction of Cameron's finger. A few hundred metres away stood a row of trees. They looked like a line of grotesque, twisted figures — ancient spirits beckoning to them, calling them to what both knew would be their final stop.

Side by side the boys wandered around clusters of thorny desert bushes, meandering towards the trees. Jamie's head was bowed and he watched his feet dragging through the sand. It was a pity for it all to be ending like this. He hoped that Eddie wouldn't search for him for too long.

"Oh my God!" Cameron had stopped dead. Jamie looked up.

The ground on the other side of the trees sloped away gently for about a hundred metres or so, then plunged into an enormous ravine, a gorge in the desert. Wordlessly the two boys made their way towards the lip of the canyon, both drawing on some new and unexpected energy source.

"Unbelievable."

The walls dropped away for what seemed like hundreds of metres but was probably only sixty or seventy. They weren't sheer, but fell in a series of narrow terraces, giant steps down into the lush canopy of trees that lined the bottom of the gorge. Bird-calls floated up to where they stood, gazing in wonderment. In the morning light the granite glowed in livid shades of red and ochre. Jagged, uneven ridges and scars ran along the sides of the valley as far as they could see. What caught their attention, though, was the trickle of deep green running between the thick forest on the valley floor. It glinted silver between the outspread branches.

"You reckon we can get down there?"

"We should give it a try, that's for sure."

The climb was perilous. They made their way along the top lip of the cliffs until they found a fracture cutting in at right angles to the valley itself.

"What do you think?"

Jamie shrugged. "Let's have a go."

Cameron led the way, testing for hand and footholds, and

Jamie followed carrying the bag. The fissure took them onto a narrow terrace about a third of the way down the face of the cliff. They moved along it cautiously, occasionally dislodging loose stones or patches of red gravel, and listening to them plummeting to the valley floor below. Soon another fracture in the rock appeared ahead of them and they continued down to the next terrace.

It took an hour of careful climbing to reach the valley floor. Twice they found themselves trapped in dead ends, and had to ascend back to the level above. When they finally stepped from the shadow of the final fault into the bottom of the gorge, they looked around in wonder.

The floor of the valley was a total contrast to the desert plain above them. Birds called in the branches of the eucalypts that formed a canopy of leaves and coloured the world green. A small creek, just a trickle of water, bubbled along only a few steps away.

"Amazing." Cameron's voice was barely a whisper.

"Yeah."

There seemed nothing more to say. They sprawled on a rock and slurped greedily at the seemingly endless supply of water. After he'd drunk his fill Cameron removed his shirt and soaked it in the water. He was just about to put it back on when he suddenly hurled it at Jamie, catching him in the chest. Jamie's look of surprise changed to one of mock determination and soon there was water flying back and forth until the two of them were soaked.

"Incredible." Cameron lay on his back, staring at the small patches of sky that showed through the leaves.

"Pretty cool." Jamie agreed.

TWENTY-EIGHT

"You know what I can't wait for?"

"What?"

"I can't wait to see the look on Butcher's face when he finds out that we're alive and we've brought the girl back with us."

They had slept the entire afternoon and right through the night. Jamie had woken first and he lay on the flat rocks by the watercourse and listened to the sound of birds calling. When Cameron surfaced they breakfasted on dehydrated noodles.

"We'll have to keep moving, you know. Otherwise we'll starve."

"Yeah." The nagging hunger was still there, even with a belly full of cold noodles.

"We should walk as far as we can along the bottom of this valley today. It seems more or less parallel to our heading from yesterday."

"When'll we climb up?" The thought of walking back into the desert, away from the cool protection of the gorge, didn't appeal to Jamie one bit.

"Late this afternoon. We can get up there for sunset, and take a bearing for our walk tonight."

The night's rest had revived Cameron's natural optimism and he had eased back into the leadership role.

They picked their way along the valley floor for two hours, clambering over rocks and fallen trees and skirting around steep outcrops that jutted into the undergrowth. In places where the scrub was too think to penetrate they waded into the creek and walked on the pebbly bottom. They discussed all sorts of things. Cameron talked about his old girlfriend back in the city, how he still kept in touch with her, and about his plans to go to uni there the following year. Unexpectedly, Jamie found himself telling Cameron all about Eddie.

"Eddie's cool, you know? It's just been pretty hard for him to get his life together, having to look out for me and all."

"So when will he be released?"

"Dunno. Depends on the parole board."

"Then what?"

Jamie shrugged. Eddie and home seemed so far away.

"I'd like him to come out here."

"Eddie?"

"Yeah. I reckon he'd like it."

A large pile of loose rocks and boulders blocked their path. It took up the whole width of the valley and the stream disappeared beneath it.

Jamie glanced at Cameron. "Up and over?"

"Sounds good to me."

The slope of the pile wasn't steep, but some of the larger stones were unstable, and it took a few minutes to scramble carefully to the top. They were unprepared for the scene that lay in front of them.

They had reached the end of the gorge. On three sides red cliffs towered into the air. Perched on the very edge, high above them, the twisted shape of a lone boab tree clung to the lip of the rocky precipice. And there, nestling at the base of the cliffs, was a deep-green pool of water, almost a perfect circle.

"Fancy a swim?"

Without answering, Jamie began to peel off his dusty clothes.

The water was freezing against their sunburned skin. Cameron began swimming across the pool in a powerful freestyle. Not as confident in the water, Jamie settled for a slow dog paddle up and down near where they'd climbed in.

Cameron came powering back. "This is so good."

"Bloody cold though."

"You'll get used to it."

Cameron floated on his back, surveying the cliffs above.

"There's only one problem."

"What?"

"No way we'll get up those walls. We'll have to head back the way we came."

"Guess we've got enough food to last till tomorrow."

"We'll have to make it last. Or else we can try and catch ..." Cameron stopped mid-sentence. "You hear something?"

Jamie went still, stunned.

There were voices coming up the valley.

"Get out, quick."

They dragged themselves up onto the rocks in a mad scramble. Cameron slipped and barked his shin.

"Shit!"

"You right?"

"Yeah. Get dressed, quickly."

By the time they'd hauled themselves into their clothes, the voices on the other side of the rock pile were clear, ringing against the valley walls.

"Who do you reckon it is?" Jamie's question went unanswered. "We oughta hide."

"You see anywhere?"

Jamie looked around. The large pile of rocks and boulders offered little concealment and behind them the pool and cliffs trapped them in a cul-de-sac.

"Nowhere to run, nowhere to hide." Cameron almost grinned at the cliche. He didn't get a chance to say anything more because at that moment two people appeared at the top of the rock pile. A guy and a girl, probably in their mid-twenties both wearing hiking boots and shorts and carrying light backpacks.

For a few seconds they stood at the top of the rocks, awestruck by the sight of the pool, much as Jamie and Cameron had been. It wasn't until they started to climb down towards the water that they realised they were not alone.

"Hi." The guy had a British accent. He seemed a little offhand, even disappointed.

"Hi ..." Cameron's voice trailed off. Jamie said nothing.

The couple reached the edge of the pool, made themselves comfortable on some rocks and, ignoring Jamie and Cameron, drank from water canteens on their backpacks. The girl started to unlace her boots and the guy took off his shirt, revealing a tanned back and chest.

"We didn't expect to see anyone down here." It was a second before Jamie realised that the man was speaking to them. "The guidebook said that this is a difficult gorge to get in to, and we thought we'd have it all to ourselves. Where are you from?"

"Port Barren." Cameron's voice sounded tired.

"Really?" The guy stopped rummaging in his bag and threw them a curious glance. "We came through there a couple of days ago. All sorts of ..." The man stopped and looked at them properly for the first time. "What are you doing out here, then?"

"We're just ..." Cameron searched for an explanation. The young woman suddenly turned to them. "You're not those two boys everyone was searching for, are you? Back in Port Barren?"

Cameron nodded. The tourists looked at one another and then back at the boys. It was the guy who finally spoke.

"What the hell are you doing way out here? They were going mad back there."

"It's a long story."

"Didn't you steal a car or something?" The young woman joined the interrogation. "We didn't see one back at the park entrance."

"Park?"

"National Park. Don't you even know where you are?"

Cameron shook his head. The guy walked across and stood directly in front of them, looking them over, taking in the fierce sunburn, the cracked lips, the puffy eyes and the filthy clothing.

"Are you okay?"

Cameron made a non-committal gesture. Sort of a shrug. Jamie stayed silent.

"My name's Robert. This is my girlfriend Susan." He nodded towards his companion. "Can we offer you guys a drink or anything?"

"You got any food other than dehydrated noodles?"

"Sure. Sit down."

He returned to his pack and dug out a couple of bars of chocolate, some potato chips, a tin of smoked mussels and some cracker biscuits.

"It's not much, I'm afraid, but you're welcome to it. We weren't planning on staying at the pool too long. The rest of our food is in the car."

"Thanks."

The boys munched hungrily. A look passed between Robert and Susan, unnoticed by Jamie and Cameron.

"So," ventured Robert. "It took us half a day to get here. How on earth did you guys manage it?"

TWENTY-NINE

The blast of the air-conditioning was a stream of paradise blowing onto Jamie's face. Cameron was in the back of the four-wheel drive, fast asleep among Robert and Susan's camping gear and backpacks. Jamie was sprawled across the back seat, his head propped on a couple of pillows Susan had found him. His eyes were closed and he was tired, but sleep refused to come. In the front, Robert was driving and Susan was sitting in the passenger's seat arguing with him.

"We ought to get them both straight back to Cameron's parents," Robert was saying. "They'll be worried sick."

"Weren't you listening to their story? The safest place for these two is the Karratha police station. The parents can be notified from there."

"They'll be okay if we take them home. I'm sure Cameron's parents are capable of dealing with this Butcher character."

"Robert" — Jamie didn't know these people all that well but he guessed from the tone of her voice that Susan was about to win this argument — "you can't just drop these boys off and leave. Not after what they ..."

"I don't want to have to deal with the police. There'll be forms to fill out and questions to answer. We're already behind schedule and you know as well as I do that if we don't get this car back to the hire company by the end of the week it'll cost us extra."

"I know that, but we've got to do the right thing."

Robert was about to be overruled. Jamie opened his eyes and spoke quietly.

"Go to Port Barren."

"What?" Susan twisted in her seat, surprised. They'd thought he was asleep. Jamie saw Robert's eyes flick to the rear-vision mirror.

"Head to Port Barren. Robert's right. Cam's parents will know what to do. We'd be better off back there than in Karratha."

Jamie was not keen to involve the Karratha police. Not yet. Not until he knew Butcher hadn't any influence with them.

"Jamie, are you sure about this?" Susan's concern was reflected in her eyes and her voice. "Have you thought it through? This man has tried to kill you once already."

"Yeah. It'll be right. I'll call the cops as soon as we get home. Cameron's father is a pretty influential guy in the town."

"Well, if you really think ..."

"You'd better make your mind up soon," Robert interrupted. "The Port Barren turnoff's only about half a kilometre down the road."

"Yeah, I'm certain. Head back to town."

A few seconds later Robert swung the Nissan off onto another dirt track. A faded sign at the intersection, almost unreadable through the dust, pointed the direction. "Port Barren — 30 km."

"Do you want us to wait around for a few minutes?"

"Nah. It'll be right."

"Good luck then. Be careful."

"Yeah, I will." Jamie stood by the passenger window. "Listen, thanks for everything. You guys saved our lives out there. We were pretty lost."

Looking at Robert's map in the car on the way home, Jamie and Cameron had realised how lucky they'd been. Not only were they still seventy-five kilometres from the nearest highway, but they had been headed in completely the wrong direction. Cameron agreed that he needed to work on his navigation skills.

"That's okay. Are you sure we can't do anything else to help?" Susan was still worried. Jamie shook his head.

"Things'll be fine. Honest. You guys should hit the road before the cops start asking around."

"If you say so. Bye then. Take care, won't you?" To his surprise, Susan leaned out and kissed him quickly on the cheek.

"See you, mate! Stay out of trouble and look us up when you get to London." Robert grinned at him from the driver's side.

"Yeah, I will. Thanks again." Jamie squeezed the address that Susan had pushed into his hand. "I'll write to you."

"Sure. That'd be great. But remember we won't be back home for another six months."

"Cool. Have a good trip."

"We will ..."

Susan's last words were cut off as Robert pulled the car out, did a three-point turn, and with a final wave, cruised slowly back down the street. Jamie watched the tail lights vanish into the dust and the darkness.

Port Barren was sleeping. The pub was closed, though a couple of lights still burned in the admin building. The uneasiness in Jamie's belly had returned as strong as ever, and his thoughts were clouded by tension and weariness.

From the pool it had been a couple of hours slow hike out of the gorge and up a side valley that the two boys hadn't even realised was there, another thirty minutes to the car park, and then a three-hour drive back to Port Barren.

Cameron had been dropped off first. He'd slept all the way

back, waking only when Jamie shook him as they passed the charred wreckage of the school. Susan tried to insist on taking him inside to his parents, but he had won out in the end, and they'd sat in the car watching him as far as the front door to make sure he got inside okay.

Jamie stood in the dust outside Archie's, feeling the customary heaviness in his shoulders and tightness in his belly. Lights burned inside the house, so Archie must still be up, thought Jamie. He was pleased that he wouldn't have to wake the old man.

He walked up the path, across the verandah and through the front door, letting the fly screen slam shut behind him with its customary crash.

"Hello?" His call hung in the air. From the kitchen came the urgent scrape of a chair and fast footsteps. Lorraine came down the hallway.

"My God! Jamie! What —" She took a couple of steps towards him, peering through the gloom, as if uncertain whether she could trust her eyes. "Where have you come from?"

"Flaherety's Curse." He watched her carefully as he said it. In the dim light of the hallway it was hard to be sure, but he thought he saw some quick emotion — fear or perhaps shock — flit across her face.

"Where?" Her voice gave her away. She knew. Jamie was sure, she had known all about it.

"You know, Butcher's dumping ground. Where he sends problems to get rid of them."

"What on earth are you talking about?"

All of a sudden Jamie felt tired. Lorraine's pretence of innocence wasn't convincing. He couldn't be bothered dealing with her.

"Forget it. We'll sort it out in the morning. When I give this to the Karratha cops." He patted the backpack and shoved his way past Lorraine.

"What? Jamie, what have you got in there?"

"An old friend of Butcher's."

He continued down the hallway towards his room on the back verandah. All of a sudden the only thing he wanted was sleep. He paused at the entrance to the kitchen. Archie was sitting in his usual spot at the table, cup of tea in hand.

"I'm back."

A nod.

"I might get some sleep. Can we have a chat in the morning?"

Another nod, this time accompanied by a curving at the edge of the eyes that might have been a smile.

"Cool." He stepped onto the back verandah and closed the door firmly behind him. Lorraine called out to him but Archie's deep tones interrupted and she went quiet. Then the front door slammed and she was gone.

Out in the back yard Jamie sluiced himself down with cold water from the tank. His skin tingled, still tender from exposure to the sun and sand. Looking up, he saw the stars peppering the sky and the moon hovering above the northern horizon. They were the same stars, in the same sky, but here in town they were somehow different from out in the desert. Jamie remembered the strange sensation that had swept through him a couple of times while they were out in the sand. The feeling of oneness, of belonging. He tried, but he couldn't recall it clearly here in town. He was aware only of the uneasiness in his mind and body, a feeling too powerful to allow that delicate sense of peace to envelop him.

He climbed the stairs, crossed the verandah, fell onto his bed, and slept.

THIRTY

"Telephone." Someone was shaking him.

Archie stood beside the bed. "You got a call. Your mate."

"Cameron?" Archie nodded. "What time is it?" But Archie had already gone.

Jamie still felt exhausted. Rolling out of bed, he retrieved his wristwatch from the table where he'd left it. (Was it only days ago? It felt like weeks.)

"Six-thirty! Jeez." He staggered up the hall in his shorts, wondering why Cameron would be calling so early.

"Yeah?"

"Jamie —" Cameron sounded worried, out of breath. "You've got to get out of there. Now."

"Huh?"

"Butcher's just left here. He's on his way to your place."

He was instantly wide awake.

"What?"

"He's been here for hours. Mum and Dad went nuts after I told them what happened, and Dad hauled him over here in the middle of the night to explain himself. They've been at it all night, him and my parents. He's denying everything, reckons you've put me up to lying to cover your own back, and he's invented some crap story about you torching the school and making me steal our car. He's on his way round to get you now. He says he'll make damn sure you tell the truth."

"Oh, shit!"

"Get out. Take it from me, you don't want to be there. He's furious."

"Where can I go?"

"Dunno. Don't come here though. My parents don't believe him, but he's been making you sound like the devil all the same."

A car pulled up. Jamie took a quick look through the front window.

"He's here."

"Run." The phone went dead in Jamie's ear.

Jamie didn't stop. He ran down the hallway. Archie stood on the back verandah with the backpack in his hand.

"She's in here, isn't she?"

"Yeah." He hadn't told Archie anything, and yet he wasn't surprised that the old man knew about the girl anyway.

"Butcher's here." The usual nod. "I reckon I might lie low for a bit."

"You be careful."

"Yeah." Jamie made for the back door.

"Jamie!"

The boy stopped and turned round. The sound of his name coming from the mouth of the old man was a new experience.

"You better take her too." Archie handed him the bag. "I've got a feeling that she's the one he's really lookin' for."

Jamie grabbed the bag and fled into the dawn.

A few streets away, he slowed down and began to move more cautiously through the town. In the growing daylight he felt exposed and vulnerable. He knew that he was probably still the most wanted man in Port Barren and that everyone in town would be happy to see him thrown in the back of the police truck.

With no destination in mind, he set about staying out of sight of the road. He ducked through a few backyards — not a difficult task given the lack of fences.

He arrived at the administration building almost without realising it. Lorraine's car was parked out the front. A quick glance showed that no one else was around, so he dashed across the street and up the steps onto the front verandah.

The door was unlocked. He slipped inside. The building was in darkness and blinds had been drawn over most of the windows. But down the far end a light burned in Lorraine's cubbyhole, and over the dull hum of the air-conditioner Jamie could hear her speaking to someone. The words were indistinct, but there was no mistaking the tone.

Ducking low to the floor, he cautiously made his way between the rows of desks and empty waste-paper baskets, easing himself to within listening distance.

Lorraine was on the phone. She was crying.

"— no idea where he is." She sounded scared. "Don't try to blame me for this. I didn't ask you to take him off. Just like I didn't ask you to get rid of the last one."

Jamie's heart thumped.

"No, I'm not going to look for him. I won't go to Cameron's place either. It's your problem this time, Elliot, you can't drag me into it. I don't care if you ..."

She stopped. Butcher was obviously speaking. Her shoulders, which had been tense and angry, slowly sagged. She looked tired and beaten. Butcher talked for some time.

"You can't ..." Her voice was choked with emotion. "It was years ago now. You can't, Elliot ..."

He cut her off again.

"It was a mistake. You can't, not after all this time ..."

A final pause, while Butcher finished whatever he was threatening her with.

"All right. Okay. If I hear anything I'll let you know. Of course."

She dropped the phone back into its cradle. Her head folded onto her arms and her body heaved with sobs.

Jamie walked to the office door.

"What was that all about?"

Startled, Lorraine leapt to her feet, knocking her chair backwards onto the floor.

"Jamie! What?"

Her eyes were red with tears, her hair dishevelled. She looked at Jamie, aghast.

"I know about the last boy. The other one."

The words took a few seconds to sink in.

"How?"

"Butcher. He told me all about it when he thought I was going to die. Is it true?"

"Is what true?"

"Did you love him?"

Lorraine came around the desk and eased herself into the old wooden school chair where Jamie usually sat.

"It wasn't like you think. It was different. He ..." She hesitated. "He needed me."

"So what happened then? If he was so special, how come you let Butcher carry him off into the desert, eh?"

Lorraine shook her head.

"I didn't ask him to. He just did it. Then he made threats — terrible threats. He said he'd arrest me. He'd tell people — newspapers."

"You didn't have to listen. You could have reported him."

Lorraine lifted her eyes to meet his.

"I wanted to, but I couldn't. I just couldn't. He'd have killed me too."

"Do you know about the girl?"

She nodded.

"Yes. He made sure I knew. He had to prove how powerful he was."

Her head sank into her hands and she began to cry again.

Jamie watched her for a couple of minutes then turned to leave.

"Jamie!" She was looking up at him again.

"What?"

"Be careful. Please."

THIRTY-ONE

Jamie ran. Steadily, he jogged along the beach and tried to fight the rising tide of panic that was swamping him, but his battered and tired body made it difficult. A kilometre or so out of town he could take no more and he slowed to a walk, glancing back nervously for signs of pursuit.

"What would Eddie do? What would Eddie do?" he asked over and over, wracking his brains to try and come up with an answer.

He was still trying to come up with a plan when the boat swum into view through the heat haze. He couldn't go back to Archie's — Butcher was waiting — and he couldn't go to Cameron's. He'd planned to get Archie and Cameron's folks to call in the cops from Karratha, and to confront Butcher, but everything had gone wrong. Things were much more dangerous now. He should have taken his chances with the Karratha cops. There was nowhere safe to hide in town and the thought of another day out in the desert held no appeal. Now here he was at the old boat, as if compelled.

At least there'll be a bit of shade, he thought. He could knick back into town tonight and call Karratha. A decision made, he sped up, anxious to make the shelter of the old wreck as soon as possible.

Under the stern of the old boat he collapsed. Across the still ocean a thin strip of dark cloud scarred the sky way out to the north. It ran from one side of the horizon to the other, a band of grey stretching as far as he could see. It was something he'd never seen before.

"Weird."

With nothing to do, his mind kept returning to the conversation with Lorraine. Butcher had her in his control, that was clear. He remembered his own words to her the night before, about taking the bag to the Karratha police. She'd have passed the information straight on, he was certain of that. The thought of what Butcher would do about it made him tremble. If he'd been a threat to the big cop before, then he was doubly so now. The fragile collection of bones, packed carefully in the bag that he was now using as a pillow, was all the evidence that existed to connect Butcher with the events of the past. It was ironic when he thought about it, that he should have brought the girl back here to the boat for protection. The very thing that had been the source of so much pain and suffering for her was probably going to save his life and let the truth about her fate finally emerge from the sands of the desert.

He'd been lost in thought for a long time when a couple of things snapped him out of his daydreaming. One was the sky. The dark cloud, which earlier had been nothing more than a smear in the distance, was moving closer and closer. It was still a long way off, but much larger, now covering a third of the sky. Brief flashes of lightning illuminated the storm from within itself and some minutes later the sound of far-off thunder rumbled across the still water. It made the old timbers of the boat tremble. As he watched and listened, fascinated by the beauty and power of the approaching clouds, something far more frightening grabbed his attention.

The police truck was speeding up the beach towards him.

*　　*

Crouched in the bottom of the boat, the sensation of déjà vu was incredible. But Cameron had been there that time and now he was alone. Almost alone — on the floor beside him lay the backpack. He could feel the girl's presence as though she were actually there in the boat with him, sharing his fear. Since they'd left the mine, her voice no longer rang in his mind. She wasn't calling to him any more, but her presence was just as strong, perhaps even more so than before. If he hadn't been so scared, he'd have found it strangely comforting.

He heard the heavy footsteps. It might have been Jamie's imagination, but inside the boat it seemed to grow darker.

"Riley!"

Butcher's shout ripped through the air like a gunshot.

"I know you're in there, son. There's fresh tracks all over the place."

Saying nothing, Jamie slipped the straps of the pack over his arms, settling the weight of the bag silently onto his back. Ready for sudden movement. Ready to run.

"We both know you're not getting out."

What were his chances of making a run for it? Butcher was overweight, and even though he was quick across a short distance he'd tire pretty fast. Then Jamie remembered the gun in its holster on Butcher's hip. He couldn't outrun a bullet.

"You might as well just come out and get it over with."

"Why don't you come in and get me, fatty?" The shout escaped Jamie's lips almost involuntarily. The question hung unanswered in the still air.

After a minute or two of waiting Jamie could take it no longer. He had to see what was happening. Butcher knew that he was in there, and so freed of the need for silence he scrambled up to the next deck, where he could at least look out through the holes in the walls.

There should have been more light coming in to the upper

deck, but now it was almost as dark on this level of the boat as it had been in the bilges. Moving aft, he peered straight up through the main hatchway. The clouds now filled the sky, rolling in from the ocean and totally blocking the sun. They boiled into one another, and the occasional flashes of lightning were much brighter than before, illuminating the inside of the boat in brief strobes. The grumble of thunder was also closer, louder, more persistent.

Edging carefully towards the bow, Jamie dropped his eye to a hole. Over at the truck Butcher had his back to Jamie as he rummaged in the small cargo space immediately behind the cab. Eventually he hauled out a large steel jerry can. It fell heavily onto the sand with a metallic clang. As he turned back, Jamie instinctively ducked again, not wanting to risk being seen, even through the tiny peephole. The dry and rotten planks would provide little protection from Butcher's gun.

The footsteps crunched towards him again. There was a splashing noise, more steps, and the acrid scent of petrol drifted through the still air. Jamie froze.

"Big storm coming." Butcher stood a little away now, shouting again. "I'd say it's the beginning of the wet. Gonna be a lot of lightning hitting this part of the coast in the next little while. Probably start a few fires around the place." The threat was clear. Crouching again at his peephole, fear gripped Jamie's belly with icy fingers.

"You throw that bag out here now and I might just be able to persuade the courts to go a little easy on you. Make sure you only get a couple of years, eh?"

It was an obvious lie. There was no way that Butcher could afford to let Jamie escape. The fumes from the petrol were doing strange things to him. His head spun. He stalled for time, desperately hoping for an idea.

"What if I stay in here?"

Butcher didn't answer, at least not with words. A quick flick of his wrist, and the flame of a zippo lighter flared in his right hand.

"I'm gonna count down from five, son. I get to zero and you're toast. Five."

"Shit!" Jamie scanned the inside of the boat, searching for an escape, a means to protect himself. There was nothing.

"Four."

"You're a dickhead, Butcher. Cameron knows all about it. He'll call the cops if I don't show up."

"Three." Another quick glance through the peephole revealed Butcher bending ponderously towards a dark trail in the sand at his feet.

"Two."

Without worrying about the strength of the deck, Jamie scurried towards the hatchway, ready to run when the flames engulfed the boat.

"One."

With an awful splintering noise the floor beneath him cracked and fell apart, and Jamie plunged back into the darkness of the bilge. On the way down his head struck something. It was just a glancing blow, but white lights exploded behind his eyes and he fell with a sickening crunch onto the sand in the bottom of the boat.

From outside there was silence. Through the dizziness and light-headedness, Jamie was aware of a soft "Whump!" and seconds later smoke began to fill the tiny, dark space.

Assisted by the petrol it took only an instant for the fire to take hold of the dry, sun-bleached timbers. The bow erupted into a column of flames and thick black smoke poured into the dark clouds. Butcher took a few steps back, a half smile on his face as he felt the fingers of heat radiate out towards him.

Inside, Jamie was drowning. A sea of dark, acrid smoke rolled over him, choking his breathing as he tried desperately to scramble back up to the top deck. He was much deeper in the hold than he had been earlier, and the roof was further away, beyond his reach. The fumes clouded his thoughts, making it difficult to get his body to respond. He tried to move forward, towards the front of the boat, where the upper deck was closer and he'd be able to climb through, but no sooner had he moved a couple of steps than he was driven back by the intense heat. He retreated deeper into the darkness towards the stern.

Staggering backwards he tripped against the remains of an engine half buried in the sand. He started to fall and braced himself for the impact.

The pain never came. Instead Jamie was being supported, his weight held up by something. He tried to see what had saved him, but the smoke, the darkness and his spinning head made whatever it was impossible to discern. Groping around, his hands grasped a bit of wood, splintered and old like the rest of the boat. And then another. Two poles, reaching up into the smoky darkness, horizontal rungs between them. A ladder. An escape.

The fire was roaring now, the sound filling Jamie's ears. As he placed his foot where he thought the first rung should be he smelt singed hair — it was his.

His body was working on autopilot. The fifth rung splintered and fell apart beneath him and he instinctively grabbed for the bulkhead above, arresting his fall just in time.

The five-second climb to the first deck took forever. Hauling himself through the hatchway he looked around desparately for an escape route. A couple of feet away, the stern hatch was the main exit for the smoke, which boiled along the roof, right above his head. A quick glance over his shoulder revealed a wall of angry, orange flame eating quickly towards him. He leapt for the hatchway and, feeling as though he was moving in slow motion, hauled himself into the open air.

He lay on the deck looking upwards, a tower of smoke racing into the sky above him. Flashes of lightning were cracking down and the roaring of the flames mixed with the crash of thunder. He crawled towards the safety rail around the edge of the boat, used it to help drag himself to his feet, and without checking the distance of the fall, he vaulted off the boat.

A burst of pain exploded in his ankle when he hit the hard dirt of the beach. He fell, rolled for a second or two, then tried to stand. Halfway to his feet his leg collapsed beneath him. The boat burned fiercely, the heat from the flames searing his skin, reminding him of the merciless desert sun. Painfully, he half crawled, half dragged himself across the ground, not worrying in which direction he headed as long as it took him away from the flames.

He closed his eyes in pain. The sand scraped at his singed arms and legs, but with each movement the radiated heat grew less and less. When he came up against something solid he stopped and looked up to see what it was. Over him stood Butcher, gun drawn.

"You're a tough little bugger. I'll give you that."

His thumb drew back the hammer. Even over the roar of the fire and the crash of the thunder Jamie heard the soft click of the bullet rolling into place in the firing chamber. He closed his eyes.

A shot rang out. The sound blended with the thunder.

THIRTY-TWO

There was no pain — no blinding flash.

Jamie lay on the sand. Waiting. But there was no searing burst of agony. No bullet tearing through his flesh.

He opened his eyes. Butcher still stood above him, but his right hand no longer held the gun. Instead his arm hung by his side, limp and still. His left hand slowly reached across and felt his right shoulder, probing at a tiny hole in the fabric of his uniform. He pulled his hand away with a jerk; a smear of blood stained his fingers. He stared at them with a puzzled expression, holding them right up in front of his face. Then his eyes rolled back in his head, and with a sickening thump he fell to the sand, unconscious.

Three figures stepped out from behind the protection of the four-wheel drive. The first was Cameron. He came straight towards Jamie, with Archie following a couple of steps behind. Finally, Constable Robb stepped into the open, holstering his service revolver as he did so.

"You okay?" Cameron crouched beside Jamie.

"I'll live. What —"

Before he could finish his question, Archie interrupted.

"Time enough for questions later."

The two of them helped Jamie to his feet. Robb was

bending over the prone shape of Butcher. Archie looked at him.

"Dead?"

Robb shook his head.

"Nah, straight through his shoulder. It's clean. He'll live."

Cameron and Archie propped Jamie on the bonnet of the truck, then Archie found the first aid kit and went to attend to Butcher. Robb spoke to someone on the radio, then swung himself up onto the bull bar, alongside Cameron and Jamie.

They sat in silence watching the fire. The boat was now engulfed, and flames leaped into the black sky like prisoners escaping confinement. The dark smoke drifted inland towards the desert.

It was a long time before the fire consumed the last of the dry wood. An ambulance arrived and there was some commotion at the back of the car as Butcher returned to consciousness and found himself under arrest. Eventually the ambulance officer sedated him so they could load him onto a stretcher.

"How did you know?"

"Where else would you have gone?" Cameron grinned at him. "Old habits die hard, eh?"

"Yeah."

After one of the ambulance officers had strapped Jamie's ankle and made sure he wasn't seriously hurt, Archie came across.

"How are you feeling?"

"I've been better, but I'll live."

"Good."

Robb spoke.

"The detective inspector's coming across from Karratha. He'll meet us back in town."

He patted his pockets as if searching for something. It was the first time Jamie had seen Robb up close without sunglasses on and he saw the same intense blue eyes as Archie's.

Finding what he was looking for, Robb pulled out a packet of cigarettes and lit one.

"When you gonna give up those poison sticks?" Archie asked, only half joking.

"When I feel like it."

"How about now?"

Robb looked at the old man, then at the packet in his hand. "Fair enough."

He took a last draw on the cigarette and flicked it towards the burning boat. It arced gracefully though the air and then blended with the larger fire. He crushed the packet and threw it in as well.

Nothing more was said. The four of them watched the burning boat slowly fall in upon itself as the flames ate through the internal timbers. Eventually, the last of the fuel consumed, the fire began to die, until the boat was nothing more than a pile of glowing embers and a couple of smoldering tyres.

From above them an enormous clap of thunder broke the stillness, and the first drops of rain fell. Fat, warm beads of water, plopping onto the sand and raising tiny steam devils in the embers.

THIRTY-THREE

"Jamie, I'm Detective Inspector Swan, and this is Detective Mueller. You up to answering a few questions?"

The two cops slouched in chairs on the other side of the desk. They looked pretty tired, but then they'd spent the last week trying to unravel the events that had culminated at the boat.

"Yeah."

"All right then. How about you tell us everything that happened, in your own words."

"From when?"

"From when you arrived."

"In Port Barren?"

"Please."

It took nearly an hour for Jamie to tell his story. He left a few things out. When the detectives wanted to know how they'd got back into town from the national park, all he told them was that they'd hitched a ride. He could tell that they didn't believe him, but they let it pass. And he said nothing about Butcher's hold over Lorraine.

It was Detective Mueller who steered the conversation towards the social worker.

"Have you heard anything from Lorraine?"

Everyone knew that Lorraine had vanished from Port Barren on the day of the boat fire.

"Nah. Have you?"

Jamie caught the look that passed between the two men.

"What?"

They obviously knew something. Swan, the inspector took over.

"They found her car late last night. She wasn't in it."

"Where?"

"Overturned in a creek, about three hundred kilometres south of Karratha. It looks like she'd tried to get across a floodway somewhere upstream but didn't make it."

Jamie could feel the eyes of the two cops on him, watching for his reaction.

"They reckon she's alive?"

Swan shrugged. "No idea. I don't like her chances though. When these desert creeks are in flood, they're pretty much unstoppable. She was stupid to even try to get across, especially in that crappy little car of hers. She probably stalled halfway, tried to get out, and got swept away."

"Will they find her body?"

Mueller answered. "Doubt it. Desert's a pretty big place."

Swan leaned across the table.

"We're still trying to work out why she ran like that. You sure you've got no idea?"

Memories of his last meeting with Lorraine, here in this very office, flickered through Jamie's mind. He also remembered the touch of her hand that night at Archie's.

"Nah. No idea. Sorry."

"Thanks Jamie. We'll need to speak to you again before we're finished here. So will a few others."

"Others?"

"There's some internal affairs people coming up from the city to investigate Sergeant Butcher."

"I'm not goin' anywhere."

The younger detective grinned. Jamie guessed they'd read his file.

"We'll be in touch." The inspector stood and held out his hand. Jamie shook it awkwardly and turned for the door, but Swan hadn't quite finished.

"Oh, yeah. There's just one more thing."

Jamie stopped.

"I nearly forgot. The forensic people wanted me to ask you — are you certain you picked up all of the remains of the girl out at the mine site?"

"Yeah."

"It's just that there's a few bits and pieces missing. Most of it can be explained by scavengers, but apparently one of the femur bones from her leg is also gone, and they're pretty big."

Jamie shrugged. "Did they look back at Flaherety's Curse?"

"I looked myself yesterday when we flew out there. Couldn't see a thing."

"Sorry. Can't help you then."

"That's okay. Just thought I'd ask."

As Jamie left, the Detective Inspector's eyes followed him thoughtfully.

Robb was waiting out on the front verandah.

"Want a ride?"

It was only a couple of minutes walk, but his strapped-up ankle still caused him a bit of pain. Besides, it hadn't stopped raining for a week.

"Thanks. Pretty heavy rain."

"Yeah. It'll come down like this through to the end of February now. Wait'll you see the desert afterwards."

"Why?"

"Everything comes to life."

Jamie tried to imagine the desert landscape alive with creeks and rivers, wildflowers and greenery. It was too difficult to picture. He'd have to wait until he saw it.

"How's Butcher?" The sergeant had been taken across to the Karratha hospital and from there he'd gone straight to the lock-up.

"Bit pissed off. Reckons he'll sort you out properly next time."

"Should I be worried?"

Robb grinned.

"Nah mate. By the time the courts finish with him he'll be lucky to get less than twenty years."

They drove the rest of the way in silence.

"Here we are. Say g'day to Grandad for me."

"Yeah. How come you don't come round more often?"

"No need. We see each other about the place."

"I guess." Jamie found it strange. He missed having his own family around. "I'll see you later, eh?"

"Yeah. Catch you."

Archie was out the back, patching a couple of leaks in the verandah roof. Jamie flopped onto his bed and watched for a while.

"Eh, Archie?"

The old man looked at him.

"You remember telling me that story? 'Bout the wanderers and the lost ones?"

Archie nodded a reply.

"I meant to ask you, what do you reckon I am?"

There was no sound but the throb of rain on tin. Archie thought about his answer for a long time, then finally he smiled. It was the first real smile that Jamie had seen on him. His teeth gleamed in the light, and his blue eyes sparkled.

"Neither mate. You're a local."

Epilogue:
A New Kind of Dreaming

The wet season passed, and the rivers and streams that had burst into life slowly dried up again. The sun returned in all its usual intensity, baking the earth and shrivelling the millions of wildflowers that had sprung up in the desert around Port Barren. Jamie had taken to running with Cameron in the mornings. They'd go off in a different direction every day. Sometimes off to the east, sometimes to the west. Now and then they'd run along the beach, passing the blackened pile of rubble that was once the boat. The place held no fear and no fascination for either of them anymore. They only ever stopped there once, about three months after the end of the wet.

"Not a lot left now."

Jamie just nodded his reply, Cameron was still by far the stronger runner, and it took him a few minutes to get his breath back.

"You ever wonder what happened to her?"

"I think the cops are still running tests and stuff."

"Yeah, that's what I heard. Seems sad, don't you reckon?"

Jamie threw Cameron a look. "Sad?"

"Yeah. She came all this way. Died like that, but didn't even get a proper burial. Not much of a welcome, is it?"

Jamie didn't reply.

A minute or so later, they resumed their run.

The pool looked almost exactly as it had the first time they'd visited. Jamie and Cameron climbed over the top of the rock pile and stood, taking in the sight of the deep green water and the cliffs rising from it. It was still breathtaking.

No words were said as they climbed carefully down to the water's edge. Cameron sat on a flat rock and shrugged off his backpack. Jamie drank deeply from his canteen.

"You're right, mate. This is the place."

"Yeah."

"They reckon it's bottomless."

"Even better, then."

Jamie also took off his pack and laid it carefully on the ground.

"Look at that." Cameron was pointing up.

The late afternoon sun caught the branches of the boab tree where it perched on the lip of the cliff. It seemed to shimmer and glow an iridescent white.

"Wow." Jamie's voice was a whisper.

"The perfect headstone, I reckon."

Jamie dug into his pack, and pulled from it a long, carefully wrapped bundle. Slowly, he peeled away the layers of cloth and padding until he held the smooth white bone in his hand.

"You want to do it?"

Cameron shook his head.

"No mate. You saved her."

Jamie threw the bone gently out into the middle of the pool. For a few seconds they could see it drifting down into the green depths, then gradually it vanished.

"Welcome." Jamie spoke the word silently.

As they climbed back to the top of the rock pile to start the long trek to where Robb and Archie waited with the car, Jamie took a last glance back. The surface of the pool was as still and unbroken as a mirror. Somewhere along the valley, a kookaburra began its raucous laughter, and at that moment the weight seemed to lift from his shoulders and belly.

"Did you feel that?" Cameron stood stock still, his voice a whisper.

Jamie nodded.

"I think she's all right now," Cameron said. "I think she's dreaming."

Jamie smiled.

"She is. A new kind of dreaming."

Grinning at each other, the two boys started back along the gorge.

YOUNGER READERS

Nathan Nuttboard
Hits The Beach

A few days at the beach, camping with your family. Sounds
like a good time, right?

Maybe, but don't forget to factor in:
the motorbike riding bogan
an older sister in love
a tent which is suffering a spiritual crisis
a surfer named Gnarly whose idea of fun involves
exfoliating sparkplugs!

For Nathan Nuttboard, this could be an interesting few
days.

*This is a fun read with lots of laughs and just enough
adventure to keep you on your toes.*

Good Reading

*Ages 7 and above won't want to put this book down until
it is finished.*

The Examiner

*An easy-to-read, humorous book that evokes instant
memories of family holidays and captures the language
of young people.*

Fiction Focus

ISBN 0 7022 3340 4

UQP

YOUNG ADULT FICTION

The Darkness

The Darkness comes for all of us eventually ...

In the small coastal town of Isolation Bay, a shadow hangs over the lives of Rohan Peters and his mother Eileen. Bound together by small town superstition, their lives are dominated by fear.

Into this setting comes Rachel, a girl on the run from her own dark history. As Rohan and Rachel struggle to build a friendship amidst the pananoia of Isolation Bay, their pasts come crashing down on them in an event that will change both of their lives forever.

"Hate isn't the most powerful emotion Rohan, people think it is but it isn't. Fear is much, much stronger ... "

An impressive debut novel. Rohan's climatic struggle with his own darkness amid the fury of the elements was as compelling as anything seen in recent Young Adult fiction.

James Moloney

ISBN 0 7022 3152 5

UQP